Furry Tales

Fins, Feathers and Whatever

Compiled by:

Jean S. Barto

ISBN 0-7414-3537-3

Published by:

INFINITY
PUBLISHING.COM

1094 New DeHaven Street, Suite 100
West Conshohocken, PA 19428-2713
Info@buybooksontheweb.com
www.buybooksontheweb.com
Toll-free (877) BUY BOOK
Local Phone (610) 941-9999
Fax (610) 941-9959

Printed in the United States of America

Printed on Recycled Paper

Published September 2006

CONTENTS

DOGS

CATS

P.S. NUMBER 60

I dedicate this book to all the animal lovers in the world.

May they always speak for the animals which cannot speak for themselves, enjoy the richness they add to our lives and never stop marveling at their unrecognized abilities.

ACKNOWLEDGMENTS

My sincerest thanks to: Camille Dawson, Mildred Hamil and Lane Heise for helping to edit this book. To Gary Heise and Jim Castellan for their computer advice. To my daughter, Lane Heise, for listening, and when asked, giving a much needed opinion concerning the item in question. To the many pet owners that gave me their stories and to all their pets.

FOREWORD

Every animal, just like people, is different. Each one has his or her distinct personality and story. Two dogs or cats from the same litter are remarkably diverse. Our brief encounter with each animal is unique, and so are the tales we tell about them.

I have found pets never object to your wind tunnel hairdo or think you look fat in your new red dress, so if you want faithful companionship and laughs, adopt a pet.

The anecdotes in this book are funny, sad, amazing and endearing. They show the sensitivity, brains and unfathomable qualities in the animals with which we have had experiences.

We are ever thankful for their place on this earth and in our hearts. The world is a better place because of them.

Dogs

"Dogs are the model for being alive."

Gilda Radner

PEPPI

By Frances Webb

I did not want a dog. David did; the children did. I said no! After months of this exchange, David came home and said, "My secretary is giving us a puppy from her litter."

I said, "No."

That night, after the two youngest, two and three, were in bed, he said to the five and seven-year olds, "Come, we're going to get a puppy."

I said, "No."

How could I? They were cheering. I did the dishes in a seething stew.

****

"Mommy, look!"

I looked. The round white ball of fur in her arms had a small black spot over its right eye and a pink ribbon around its neck.

"Isn't he cute?"

"Hmmmmmm."

"We're naming him Pepperoni."

"Better let your sisters in on the naming." I walked back into the kitchen.

It whimpered.

"Did you put him down? Pick him up." I called and visually laid newspapers all over the floor, covered all the furniture, put plastic on the walls, hid my shoes.

"Come on," David said, "we'll go up and show him to your sisters."

Yes, I thought, and you will never be forgiven for not taking them along, too.

****

(I was right. Those sisters are now in their late forties, and they have not forgotten that).

****

The next day, David went to work, the two oldest went to school and the two youngest cuddled and fed Peppi (renamed).

I won an argument about making him stay in the kitchen. I picked up wet newspapers and put down dry ones over and over. I said, "Don't fill its water bowl...too full; its water bowl is empty...it needs lots of water. Don't just keep feeding it...it should eat only at mealtime...remember what Daddy said about that." They cuddled it, so I did not need to.

The next day, a Saturday, David took all four shopping with him.

The white ball of fur, still in its pink ribbon although a boy, and I looked at each other. "Okay," I said. "See this newspaper? I'm going to gradually move it toward the door and you'd better follow it."

It did not follow.

I pulled the newspaper with the dog on it toward the door. It piddled. Good. Did it understand? No, probably fear made it go. I picked the ball up and pulled the wet newspaper out from under it. Its legs seemed way too short and way to flimsy for the amount of ball on top of them. I put it down on clean newspaper and it snuggled into the crook of my bent knee. I stood up, which meant he had to unsnuggle. "Lie down," I said, "and go to sleep. I'm off to make the beds."

I left the kitchen, closed the door and started toward the stairs.

Was that whimpering? Yes. Oh dear! The whimpering became crying. It got louder the further from the kitchen I got. This puppy was NOT going to be spoiled. Nor was I going to take it under my care. I was on the third step of the stairs, and hearing the now loud crying .Yes, I would feed it and train it when the REAL owners were not around. That crying would be a bark, if there were a bigger body pushing the sound from it. It would have to be clear to this puppy that I was NOT a source of affection. There were plenty of others to do that job, ones who wanted to do that job.

I was at the top of the stairs now, and finally the distance was drowning out the sound. Or…was it? Was that now whimpering again? Had the almost bark gone back to being a whimper? Yes, and that meant that the puppy had given up.

I stood, my hand on the banister. He had given up hoping that someone would come to him. To not respond to a cry was difficult, but to not respond to the silence after the crying had stopped, was painful. I pushed the kitchen door open. I scanned the floor for the ball of white fur. Not there! Not there? I got down on my knees. Nothing. "Peppi"…. Then my face began getting licked and tiny feet began searching for footholds in my skirt.

"Okay, okay…" It snuggled. This time the snuggle was in my lap, and I could not walk away from it. I would have to get up. And dump it? Yes, dump it. I had work to do, those beds.

The feet found their footholds. The beds could wait probably. Nobody really cared if their beds were made or not. But breakfast needed cleaning up. I slid my hand under the stomach. It squirmed and then snuggled harder. I pulled

4

my hand out. I watched my hand as it traveled across the fur toward the head. It looked as though I was going to pet the head. That did seem to be what I was doing...but enough was enough. "Up you go." It plopped onto a newspaper.

I got up, picked up an egg plate and went to the sink. I turned on the water and let it run on the plate. Something was on my foot. I looked down. Yes, something was! Some white fur...a ball of it.

I put the plate on the counter and turned around to get another one. I moved my foot and the ball got up. I put it down one step away, and the ball got on it. I picked it up for the next step, and the ball got up. I put it down to finish that step, and the ball got back onto it.

I leaned over and tried to explain...about requirements for walking. It licked my chin. I stood up and put one foot on top of the other foot while I quickly stacked the rest of the plates. I looked down. It had climbed up my feet and was on the top of the second foot, his tail hanging toward the floor and his toes clinging to my shoelaces.

"I give up!" I picked him up and tucked him under my arm, picked up the stack of plates and stepped over to the sink. I put the plates into the sink. And then set him on the floor. He lay down on my foot again before I could stand up straight.

****

"Mommy, we're home. How is Pepperoni?... Mommy, where's Pepperoni?... Mommy, did you..."

"I thought his name was Peppi? He's right here, on my foot."

The girls ran into the kitchen, looked down at my foot and said, "Daddy, come look!" David came in. He looked at my foot, then at the girls. They turned to look at him. He winked, and said, "Guess we did it."

SADIE

By Jean Van Wart

Sadie was a black, white and brown, mid-sized dog; not a Cocker, Boxer, Collie or Retriever, just a dog dog. We loved her, in spite of the fact that she wasn't exactly valedictorian of her dog school class. She loved a car ride and went everywhere with us.

One day, Sadie and I did some errands, Sadie sitting like a queen on the front passenger seat observing everything that went by. I pulled into a carwash. Sadie wagged vigorously at the cashier, then resumed her regal position on the front seat. Windows up, car in neutral, we advanced into the torrential cavern, the water pelted the roof and windshield. Sadie, ever alert and fascinated, seemed to enjoy the splashing around her. The rinse ended, vacuums started and we pulled out into the sunlight. Sadie stood up and thoroughly shook herself, as she always did after a complete drenching, then resumed her position. No wet fur for her. Did I say she wasn't valedictorian?

THE PROBLEM SOLVER

By Lane Reed Heise

I never fall asleep in the vet's waiting-room, there is too much going on. As I sat there, my two cats ogled nervously the English Bulldog leaning against his snaggle-toothed owner. A Pitbull Terrier sneered at my cats while two Yorkies argued over a mitten on the floor. All this made for interesting viewing, when a woman rushed in with her Beagle and headed for the reception desk. All eyes were on the new arrivals.

"Do you have an appointment?" the receptionist asked.

"Oh, yes, my name is Mrs. Brown and this is Barney. I called this morning. Barney has been constipated for a week!" she declared loudly and with emphasis.

"Wait just a minute," the receptionist said and left.

Meanwhile, Barney had settled patiently in the middle of the floor, sizing up friends and foes. Shortly after, the doctor's assistant appeared at the desk. "Mrs. Brown, you say your dog has been constipated for a week? Are you sure?"

"Absolutely!"

"Have you given him any laxatives, and if so what?" the assistant asked.

"Well, yes, many but no luck," she responded.

"Mrs. Brown, I don't think you need us."

"But we do," Mrs. Brown pleaded, "please help us!"

With that, laughter erupted in the waiting room. Mrs. B. turned. All the animals had snapped to attention. Barney had solved the week's problem himself in the middle of the waiting room floor.

WHAT WE DO FOR OUR FRIENDS!
By Jean S. Barto

Sitting comfortably in a local restaurant, a friend, Helen, and I waited for her roommate to join us for dinner. We chatted about what we'd been doing and about their four-legged trio: Daisy, a Dalmatian; MacGregor, a Scottie; and Tootsie, a plain old, sociable cat. They were an odd threesome but best friends.

Joan arrived a few minutes later and we exchanged the 'How are you, and what have you been doing' pleasantries. It looked like it was going to be a fun evening. Joan then turned to Helen and asked, "Did you remember to turn on the TV when you left?"

A stricken look wiped the calm, friendly expression off Helen's face. "No, I forgot!" A withering look flashed from Joan's eyes.

"Why would you turn on the TV when you are not there?" I asked innocently. They both looked at me like the village idiot had just joined them.

The answer was "The 'trio' likes to watch 'Animal Planet'.

Doesn't everyone?

BOYS' BEST FRIEND

By F.F. Parry, Colonel, USMC (Ret)

In the spring of 1956, I was stationed in Richmond, Virginia with responsibility for the local U.S. Marine Corps Reserve Battalion. We lived north of the city, a few blocks from the busy U.S. Route #1. My wife and I had five sons, ages 13, 11, 8, 5 and 3. The youngest, Mike, was mentally retarded.

It was a beautiful day and my sons and I had a softball game in progress. Mike and our three year old German Shepherd, Ronno, were watching the action. As the game became more spirited, we failed to notice that Mike had drifted away. Soon Ronno became agitated and started tugging on the batter's pants. We told him to go away, but he insisted, even more vigorously. It dawned on us that he wanted us to follow him. We then realized that Mike was missing. Off he loped down towards Route #1 with me and the older boys in hot pursuit. The usual profusion of trucks and cars were hurtling by at sixty miles an hour. There was Mike, in front of us, a half a block from Route #1 and heading determinedly for the noisy, dangerous highway. I was able to reach him just in time.

It is useless to speculate what would have happened if this innocent, three year old tyke had wandered out into this deadly traffic. But it couldn't have been anything good.

So our faithful animal friend, who loved all the boys and was beloved by them in turn, sensed the danger and alerted us in time to save his little friend.

Semper Fidelis!

COOKIE
By Doris Conklin Mackenzie

It was a very hot day in August 1989. I was on my way to an appliance store to buy a fan. Instead of going my usual route to the front of the mall, I went by way of the rarely used back service entrance where I knew I could find a parking place. As I was heading down the road, I happened to spot a little black dog trotting along the sidewalk. At the time, I remember wondering where his owners were, but I guess I just assumed they were probably at the garage I had just passed. After I made my purchase and was heading home, I saw the same little dog. This time a woman was leaning over talking to him. I was happy to see them together so I stopped the car and called out, "I'm glad you found your dog."

She looked up and said something which I couldn't hear, so I parked the car, got out and walked over to her.

"This isn't my dog," she said, "I come here as often as I can and bring him some food and water. I would love to take him home with me, but I can't because I live in an apartment." She went on, "I wish I knew where he came from, but I have an awful feeling that someone must have just dumped him here and left him. He's been at this spot all by himself for at least three months. Look over there," she said, pointing to where he was sitting in a little indentation in the hedge. "That's his place where he sits most of the day. I think he's waiting for the people to come back for him."

I just looked at the lady, absolutely horrified. I could not believe that anyone could be that cruel to a helpless little animal.

She told me she guessed that he had somehow managed to survive by eating out of trash cans around the mall, and by getting leftover chicken legs from the men up at the garage. "As often as I can, I bring him some food and water."

I sat down on the curb and put my hands behind me. Suddenly I felt a wet tongue on my hand. I turned around and saw this little black, furry dog looking straight into my face. I melted. I put my arms around him and hugged him.

"Can you take him home?" she asked.

I wanted to. Oh my, how I wanted to, but I knew I had better not. My husband, Joe, (who was away on a business trip at the time) believed that our one "big black dog" was quite enough! Plus, at the moment we were also taking care of our daughter's dog, another "big black dog."

I said, "I can't. I wish I could, but I can't, I really can't."

Finally, reluctantly, I said goodbye and left the two of them there. The lady was walking back to her car, and the little dog was sitting in the hedge, all alone. By the time I got home, ten minutes later, I was almost in tears and I knew I had to go back for him.

Once that was decided, I moved quickly and called our vet. It was a Wednesday afternoon, and I knew they were normally closed for staff meetings, but I was determined to get their help. I talked as fast as I could. I explained the situation. I know I became emotional, but I didn't care. I told them that he'd been all alone for three months, and that some rotten, cruel people had just dumped him off, and he was eating out of trash cans and eating chicken bones, etc., etc. I went on and on without stopping. Finally, in desperation I'm sure, the person interrupted me saying, "Go get him, we'll check him out."

Fast as I could, I grabbed a leash and collar and zoomed back to the mall. I rounded the corner past the garage and saw him just where I'd left him, sitting all alone in his little "home in the hedge." I parked, went over close to him and tried to coax him to come to me. I think he was scared because he kept skittering away. I couldn't catch him. I had nothing to grab onto. I was getting desperate. Then I noticed a man pushing a broom on the side of the road. He called over to me, "You tryin' to catch that dog?"

"Yeah," I answered, "But as you can see, I'm having no luck."

"Want some help?" When I said "I sure do!" he came over to where I was. The little dog ran out to meet him.

Okay," he said. "Just do what I say." He laughed when he gave me my instructions. "You sit on the curb and then 'bounce' down the hill." Sounded strange to me, but I said, "OK."

He knows me," he said, "so he'll follow me and we'll catch him at the bottom of the road." With that he called to the dog, "C'mon Bill," Sure enough, the little guy followed him. I did like I was directed and 'bounced' down, and together we caught him at the bottom of the hill. We managed to get the collar and leash on him. And I put the poor terrified little dog in the car. I thanked the "street sweeper" profusely for all his help, then headed to the veterinarian. The whole way he was shaking like a leaf. I kept telling him that he would never be hungry or lonely again, but he was too scared to understand. Dr. Fox greeted us as we entered his office. He patted his head and said, "Okay, little guy, let's see what's up." After about an hour, he pronounced him as healthy as could be and probably under one year old. We were both amazed. He also commented about what a nice dog he was.

Relieved, I took him home and Doodle and Dexter welcomed him as if he was their long lost buddy. After they all wagged their tails and sniffed each other, Cookie officially became a member of the family. By this time he also had a new name, "Cookie," (obviously because be was such a "smart little cookie," to have survived the way he did).

The next day I went back to the mall. I wanted to leave a sign for the lady who had taken care of him. I knew she would worry when she saw that he was gone. The sign said, "To all of you who cared for the little black dog that has been here for three months. He has a new home with people who love him, and grandchildren who will love him, and another dog to play with. Thank you. From Cookie's new family."

I pushed the stick attached to the sign into the ground of his "home in the hedge" and hoped that she would see it and be relieved knowing that he was safe.

Meanwhile, back at home, the three dogs and I were happy as larks with each other, but Cookie still had to pass his final test – his new "father" – who was due home in a couple of days. (Joe and I talked on the phone nearly every night, but I had deliberately refrained from mentioning that there was a new four legged addition to his family. After all, he had announced quite a few times, "One dog is enough!") Well, Friday arrived and Joe returned from his trip at about eight o'clock at night. Doodle and Dexter and Cookie heard his car and ran to the door to greet him. They were all

to cavort with any children passing the house. However, dinnertime always brought him to the doorstep.

One cold fall day, he did not return for the evening repast. Oh, well, we thought, he'll be home soon, but the hours went by, and days were consumed by our concern. We posted signs, advertised in the local paper, but to no avail. Two weeks went by with no sign or word about Lucky.

One Sunday night, biting winds were blowing, the clock had just struck eight times. Alone in the living room, I heard a faint scratching at a side French door. I thought it must be the wind, but soon I heard it again. I opened the door. Lucky fell in at my feet. He was dirty, his coat matted and his paws bleeding where the skin had been worn off.

Answering my shrieks, the whole family gathered. My father picked him up, laid him in his bed and tended to his wounded feet, while we ran for water and food. For two days, he slept almost around the clock. We would hand feed him, pick him up, carry him to the nearest tree, and then put him back in his bed. Slowly he started to recuperate.

Where had Lucky been? Why was he so debilitated and wounded? The only scenario that seemed plausible was that someone had picked up this friendly tailwagger and taken him a long way from us. Given a chance, he must have escaped and started his long odyssey home.

The little tramp recovered and traded his wanderlust for a soft spot on the sofa. We were the lucky ones!

THE CALMING EFFECT
By Richard Hudome

Before my sister, Doris, was married, I was waiting for Don, my future brother-in-law in his living room when his Cocker Spaniel, named Pedro, ran out of the kitchen like he was shot out of a gun. He raced through the dining room, into the living room, over the top of the sofa and up the stairs to the second floor. I had never seen the dog before and was totally astonished! Don said that Pedro would from time to time exhibit this form of behavior. I suppose this was due to the fact that he was alone in the house on certain days and this was an energy release expression.

In any event, at a subsequent date, Don came home and went directly up to the attic to retrieve something stored there. Pedro, with his usual exuberance, came flying up the stairs, across the attic floor and straight out of window left open for ventilation! Fortunately for Pedro, even though that window was three stories up, he landed in a flowerbed. The veterinarian said he had no broken bones or internal injuries. However, Pedro became a much calmer dog and lost his desire for explosive romps.

PHONETIC INTERPRETATION
By Richard Hudome

At a time when I was managing a furniture store in Malvern, Pennsylvania, one of our delivery men, who was a motorcycle enthusiast with the usual black leather jacket and numerous tattoos, acquired a puppy. When I asked what he had named his dog, his reply was "Deeo'ggee." I said that is an unusual name, how did you happen to name him that and how do you spell it? Some of you reading this probably already know the answer. His reply was "D O G."

SCUBA DOG

By Richard Hudome

Our family lived adjacent to the Cobbs Creek Golf Course in Delaware County, Pennsylvania. We had a female Wire-Haired Terrier named "Rags." I frequently took her to the golf course for a run. I would locate a suitable stick and throw it. She would race after it and immediately return it for the usual verbal reward, as well as the pat on the head. She then anxiously awaited the next throw. Then, one day I started throwing it into the creek and she always returned with the stick.

At some future time I apparently picked up a water-logged stick and threw it into the creek. Down it went to the bottom. She jumped in and could not find it. Suddenly her head disappeared and only her three-inch tail was visible. When she didn't pop up, I began to worry, but a few seconds later her head reappeared with the stick and returned for her usual rewards. This swim was repeated on several occasions, but only one time per trip. I did not want to drown her.

LIFE IN THE FAST LANE

By Nancy Puhl

The Greyhound is the fastest dog in the world. They are members of the dog grouping called "sight hounds," which also includes Whippets; which can actually go sometimes faster than Greyhounds for a longer time, but it takes them longer to build up speed. Other speedy sight hounds include Borzois, Salukis and Afghan Hounds, to name but a few. The Afghan are great jumpers. They can jump a five foot fence from a standing position.

All dogs also have an outstanding sense of smell, 50,000 times greater than a human. But through centuries of training Greyhounds have learned to rely more on their eyesight. The reason the breed was developed to hunt by sight was due to the terrain. The Greyhound originated in the Middle East where the terrain was wide and flat. He then could chase down an animal on the horizon at blinding speed. That speed has been already clocked at 43 miles an hour for a half mile, almost as fast as a racehorse and twice as fast as a human. For this reason, Greyhounds can never be let off a leash unless in an enclosed controlled area. They will not come when called if frightened or busy chasing a prey.

The Greyhound's body has basic characteristics designed to enhance its speed; long legs, narrow head, deep chest, sloping hips and, in many cases, webbed feet, much like the foot of a rabbit, its prey. The webbing provides more force. My Greyhound, Hoss, has webbed feet. Even though adopted Greyhounds are neutered, they do not seem to overeat and get fat. They may add some weight in retirement but you can still see the outline of the ribs. Although as they age, they may get arthritis. Hip dysplasia, a typical problem for retired Shepherds and Retrievers, is never a problem for Greyhounds.

They also have a fast metabolism and fewer fat cells than other breeds. Therefore, there is less pressure on joints. The disadvantages are: first that they need special shelter from the heat of summer and cold of winter. They must wear coats when the thermometer is down at freezing. The second is this breed is valuable in research laboratories. The veins are not hidden and blood can easily be extracted. Many greyhounds have made great contributions often at the cost of their lives to medical and military research. Their mild temperament allows them to submit to almost any type of pain and remain tractable; because of this many have been badly abused. It takes much less anesthesia for a Greyhound that may need it, and it still takes longer for recovery. With all medication, they need a lighter touch. A French poet, who raised Greyhounds, Alphonse de Lamortine (1790-1869) wrote to a friend saying that many doctors at the time were killing Greyhounds by accidentally giving too much medicine, thinking they were dogs when in fact he called them "four-legged birds."

Greyhounds, however, are not always universal blood donors, as often thought, but if they have blood types 1.1+ and 1.2+ then they are often used as donors. There are thirteen different canine blood types. Ninety-nine percent of dogs have 4+. Many Greyhounds do have this special 1.1+ or 1.2+ blood needed to be a donor.

My Hoss, the dog I have at present, had a chance to be a hero last summer. A Labrador Retriever was being treated at the vet's office. He had had a serious operation and needed a transfusion to help him pull through. Hoss became the donor that saved this dog.

Greyhounds are valued for what they can do, admired for how they look but most of all loved for the way they are. I have had altogether six Greyhounds. At one time I walked four at a time. I have just one now, Hoss. Cue, my first, was a real people person, as well as a lap dog. Dolly was an escape artist, but she also loved children. Greyhounds are not usually territorial at all. Hoss seems to be the most territorial of any that I've had. He does not like to be outside unless I'm also there. He does not try to run the fence, but comes right back to the door to come in even in nice weather.

Animals seem to understand everything that is said to them in almost any language. A really stellar example of this was an experience I had with my first Greyhound, Cue. It was Christmas time. I had decided to visit my niece near Albany and a friend in Agawam, Massachusetts. Since Cue was a wonderful traveler, getting along well with all people and animals, I decided that he should go along. It worked out very well.

In Agawam, there had been a snow storm before we arrived and the roads, especially the side streets, were very icy. On an especially nasty night my friend and I had decided to stay in for the evening. At bedtime, however, the dog needed to be walked. I put his coat and leash on him and we bundled up for our walk. It was dark and very icy, due to a light sleet that was falling. We had gone about halfway down the block. It was miserable trying to avoid the really icy spots in the dark. I commented aloud, "Well, Cue, I hope you'll let me know when you want to go back because it's really nasty out here." I had hardly finished the statement when Cue turned himself abruptly around to go in the opposite direction. I hadn't expected such a sudden and definite response.

Because Greyhounds tend to be double jointed, they often sleep like a bird or a cat. Cue usually slept with his paw behind his ear.

Greyhounds are sometimes used as therapy dogs because they are so gentle. When Cue and Dolly were alive they almost always went along when I visited shut-ins.

They were also official Ambassadogs once a month at the Make Peace with Animals Greyhound Center in Doylestown, Pennsylvania.

****

Another Greyhound story happened at Christmastime in 1999. At the time I had three greyhounds; Cue, Dolly and Red. I had decided to give the dogs new beds for Christmas, as well as fancy red velvet ruff collars to wear on Christmas. I never thought about whether they would like them or not, just thought they would look festive for the holiday, especially the Christmas Eve party at my house. When I took the special collars from the package, I announced to the hounds that these were to make them look handsome. I laid them on the bench with the other dog coats. As always, Christmas is a very busy time so the last few days I was out shopping or decorating to get the house and me ready for Christmas Eve.

Red was a very shy dog and spent most of his time up on the floor in my bedroom while the other two were downstairs. On Christmas Eve day, I went to get the collars to put on the dogs. One seemed to be missing. I looked all over the room for it, looked high and low, to no avail. I was really puzzled. The other collars did not look like they had been disturbed. For some reason I went upstairs, probably to get Red's dinner pan to clean it, and what to my wondering eyes did I see but the special Christmas collar placed lovingly on top of his stack of treasures. It had not been chewed or hurt in any way. He wanted to make sure he got his and that no one damaged it.

Technical and historical information was taken from:
Branigan, Cynthia A. "The Reign of the Greyhound." (A Popular History of the Oldest Family of Dogs). New York: Howell Book House, 1997.

OUR CANINE SECURITY SERVICE
By Nancy Puhl

During my time working for the government in Europe, I had many experiences with animals. In France, my friend rented an old farmhouse (1863) just along the Maginot Line outside Verdun. We had a second floor apartment with an eat-in kitchen and a wooden floor. It was very special because of the working fireplace which helped warm us in the winter. The only entrance to this apartment was up the steps in the attached barn.

We decided to adopt Miniature Poodles from a military family on base, who raised AKC registered ones. I have always loved dogs. We picked a brother and step-sister,

21

Pierre and Suzanne. They were company for each other while we taught. In Europe people travel with their animals, especially smaller ones. They even go into restaurants, as long as their papers are kept up-to-date, and we took them. More importantly, we both owe these dogs our lives.

It had been a cold week in February. New snow had fallen in the Vosges Mountains. What a great time to ski on our favorite mountain Gerardmer over the week-end. We planned to leave after school. We were so lucky because the daughter of our landlady, Pounette, had befriended us and didn't mind lending a hand with the dogs. We hadn't mentioned our plans to leave on Friday to Pounette and her husband. Upon returning to our apartment after school, we realized our error. Pounette had a blazing fire in the kitchen and had left a wonderful pigeon casserole on the coal stove. Normally, the coal stove was the only heat in the kitchen. Oh well, we'd leave early on Saturday morning and alert Pounette of our intentions. There might still be time for skiing Saturday afternoon and Sunday.

We had Pounette's pigeon pie dinner in front of the roaring fire. We had seldom seen such an immense log as the one Pounette had chosen for the fire. We hated to leave that cheery kitchen, but we wanted to get an early start in the morning. This fireplace had a metal screen that could be pulled down at bedtime. This cut off the air to the fire so it would slowly go out. Sometimes the fire could start again in the morning just by lifting the metal screen. We planned to just leave it down, so we went to bed.

Although our dogs had beds of their own, they usually preferred to sleep on or in our beds. On this particular night they had not been inclined to leave the warmth of the kitchen. About two or three hours after we had retired, we were awakened by loud barking. The dogs were racing back and forth wildly between the kitchen and the bedroom. Upon entering the kitchen, we could see why the dogs were barking. The kitchen seemed smoky. This seemed strange as the fireplace was closed but maybe not all the way. We pushed the door down harder and opened the windows to clear out the smoke. When we went back to bed the dogs decided to join us on our beds. We had no sooner gotten to sleep when that whole charade began again, the barking and running back and forth from the bedroom to the kitchen. This time there was less smoke. I could actually see that it was not coming from the fireplace now, but seeping slowly up between the floorboards in the kitchen. Oh gracious! The fireplace below us must be on fire, I thought.

I ran downstairs and outside to bang on the door of the renters, a young military couple with a young baby. They were not pleased at all at my banging. "Your apartment is on fire!" I screamed at them.

"No, it's not ours. It must be yours," they replied.

I returned to find the smoke getting much stronger. My friend, Paulene, was frantically filling pails of water at the sink and dumping them into the fireplace. The dogs continued running and barking at us. We had no phone in the apartment. "Since you have your coat on already, run up to Pounette's house and call the Pompiers," (France's answer to the volunteer fire brigade) Paulene yelled, as I started to come in again. I ran to the end of the street.

Pounette and Andre insisted on returning to the apartment with me, but first Andre had to stop at his friend's house to get the help of the fire department. Pounette and I raced ahead to do what we could. Paulene was still emptying pans of water onto that giant log which was still smoldering. The open windows made it very cold now in the kitchen. It wasn't long before Andre arrived with the fire brigade, no clanging engines just two men with a very old garden hose. Luckily there was a spigot in the garden just below the windows. They attached the hose there and tried to throw it up and in the window. All they achieved was a wet window sill. Change of plan, the hose was brought into the apartment and attached to the kitchen sink. The floor was completely hosed down especially near the fireplace. The firebricks were still hissing from the extreme heat of the fire and the chill of the water. It seems that the firebricks were so old and the log was so big that the heat from the burning had seeped down to the main support beam and it was smoldering.

What was left of that big log had to be removed, of course. Pounette and Andre said they would contact a mason they knew to rebuild the entire fireplace. For most of that week, we had an enormous hole in the kitchen floor that looked down into the apartment below. We put stools and chairs around the hole so the dogs wouldn't fall in while we were at school. We didn't want to fall in either.

If it had not been for our dogs, Pierre and Suzanne, I might not be here to tell about this. That weekend we celebrated the dogs. They sat politely in chairs at the table with us, and we all had ice cream and cake. They looked like proud little people. They seemed to know what they had done and that we were proud of them.

PASHA

By Karen Markey-DeMuro

Pasha was my male German Shepherd whom I raised from the age of seven weeks. People often mistook Pasha for a female because of his name ending in an 'a'. Pasha is a term for a man of high rank in the Turkish government. It was the name of the first stallion I ever rode, and because my puppy was from a 'p' litter, which is a common means in Germany for registering a litter, by the letters of the alphabet, I decided to use it to name my puppy.

My profession during the years I had my dog was working at a horse farm where they did breeding and also boarded various show horses. The farm was more than 100 acres and required much maintenance during all seasons.

24

Pasha went to work with me everyday and almost never spent time in the house except when I waitressed at night and on Saturdays.

His first three years, Pasha and I trained on a search and rescue team which provided volunteer canine search teams whenever needed. He could no longer participate on the team when, at age three, it was determined that he had an illness of the pancreas. With the help of my horse vet, I was able to control Pasha's disease through pills and diet.

Again we resumed our normal routine of working on the farm everyday. I never needed a collar and leash for Pasha. He never wandered from me and everyone knew where I was because Pasha would always sit outside the door to any room where I would be. The loyalty of a German Shepherd is certainly unmatched. They are a breed loyal to their person of choice and much to my mother's dismay the one person in a German Shepherd's life comes first. Camping trips, vacations and daily trips to the park included Pasha.

I remember a day when I was taking care of a few horses at a farm whose owners were away on vacation. I left Pasha outside the barn while I fed them, because of an anti-social dog they had inside the barn. When I finished feeding the horses, I came outside to find Pasha was missing. Calling his name around the farm and up and down the nearby street was fruitless. After one half of an hour, I started to panic. My fear was that if someone found Pasha they wouldn't know how to care for his disease and he could die as a result. I called a friend at 6:30 a.m. to come help me look for my missing dog. About an hour passed, I could even hear a few construction workers down the street join in calling for Pasha. I was overwhelmed with sadness and could not imagine going on with everyday life should I not find him. Finally while walking up the street scanning both sides, I saw my dog in a fenced in yard sitting and staring at me. Opening the gate, Pasha started barking incessantly and wagging his tail. I could have shaken him for not barking to let me know where he was. What a relief! I never let him out of my sight after that experience.

I had about five additional years with Pasha until I lost him to cancer in December, 2004. Shortly after his death, I purchased another male German Shepherd named Odin. My working situation has changed since Pasha. I no longer work at the farm. My husband and I take Odin on daily walks and allow him freedom of the house and yard. Odin could never replace Pasha, but has filled the void in my heart and empty space in my truck. As Odin matures, I have observed in him the similar traits of loyalty, intelligence, agility and beauty that existed in Pasha. Anyone who owns a German Shepherd and includes them as a member of the family, would have to agree that German Shepherds are wonderful animals.

THE WAYS OF LOVE

By Betty Corrigan

Dodie, a silver Miniature Poodle, was only three when her world caved in. The family that had loved and cared for her could no longer keep her. The couple planned to move into an apartment and, in addition, they were expecting a baby. Knowing this would complicate Dodie's walking schedule made the decision to give her up easy. This brought Dodie to her knees.

The couple knew an older man who had had and lost Fancy, a Miniature Poodle that he loved dearly. They thought he would provide a good home for her, so they offered her to him. However, Dodie's run of bad luck was not over yet. The man could not take her, but he did suggest me, his stepdaughter and my husband, as possible foster parents for Dodie. We had loved Fancy, so it was not a tough decision to adopt this little orphan.

Dodie moved in. We played with her, walked and fed her, stroked her and moved her bed into our bedroom so she not would feel lonely. It turned out to be a happy arrangement for the three of us. In a month or so her black button eyes told us she was "home."

One morning, soon after Dodie's arrival, my husband noticed he had a black sock missing. I searched the washing machine (the notorious sock-eater), the dryer, the floor, everywhere – no sock. A few days later, the errant sock appeared in Dodie's bed with her preferred toys. There she was, looking sheepish, with a proprietary paw covering it. I didn't have the heart to take it from her. The next morning I found the sock downstairs behind the chair on which she had staked a claim – her favorite chair. There it stayed until bedtime. When it was time to go upstairs, we called, "Come, Dodie, it's time to go to bed." The little silver bullet ran behind "her" chair, picked up the sock, streaked upstairs and dropped it in her bed.

For the next eight years until Dodie died, she followed the same routine, hiding the sock behind "her" chair during the day and taking it upstairs to her bed every night. She loved her other toys, but she slept closest to the black sock. We always thought this was her way of saying, "I love you for adopting me."

PUPPY'S REVENGE

By Ann Cline

Approximately seven months old at the time, our Heinz 57 variety mutt from the SPCA decided to lift his leg on the dining room carpet. Perturbed and anxious to correct this bad behavior, my husband, Ted, promptly swatted the dog's rear end while loudly exclaiming, "NO!" Tugger sped off into the living room to sulk. We sat back down to finish our lunch, determined to clean up the mess later.

Not more than 20 seconds later, Tugger made his next purposeful appearance. He made a beeline to the table, but this time he lifted his leg directly on Ted's foot. So there! It was a good thing for Tugger that our anger turned quickly into laughter, and it was a good thing for us that Tugger gave us 12 years of wonderful "dog" companionship after this isolated (guess we know who's boss) incident.

THE MARVELOUS MINIS

By Edith Williams

Our two long-haired miniature Dachshunds are agility trained dogs; Milton S. Hershey, eight years old and Milton's Magnificent Marilyn Monroe, five years old. They train on obstacle courses at the Y2K9s Sports Training Club in Wyndmoor, Pennsylvania, and have been competing for several years.

Now, Monroe is a Flyball Champion too, and has the ribbons to prove it. Flyball races have not quite made it to the Penn Relays or Milrose Games, but who knows maybe the Olympic Committee will be scouting them someday.

Flyball competition pits two teams of four against each other. Each of the four dogs has to hurdle four jumps ten feet apart (the height to be determined by the shortest dog). Monroe's jumps are at eight inches high. After the four jumps, each dog has to jump onto a wooden box which releases a tennis ball. Back over the four jumps, ball in mouth, the dog gives it to the handler. Then, the next dog on the team runs.

The team can be made up of a Dachshund, Dalmatian, Doberman and Deerhound; possibly pitted against a Beagle, Borzoi, Bloodhound and Bulldog, or even a Cockapoo, Border Collie, Chihuahua and Chow, whatever. The trick is to pick a start dog for endurance, the second and third dogs must be dependable and solid, and the fourth one fast as a Kentucky Derby filly and as competitive.

Every Friday night there is team practice for the Philadelphia Barking Authority at theY2K9's club. Once a month a competition is held anywhere from New England to North Carolina and off we go, the eager dogs and their trusty owner/handlers.

Although Milton does not participate in the Flyball races, he shines as a Rydal Park (life-care facility) Therapy Dog. On holidays, he and the other dogs are dressed up for the occasion. Birthday parties have been held for the dogs and even a Prince Charming contest during Monroe's Princess party.

Milton also writes a column for Y2K9s. "Magic Moments by Milton." His articles and photos feature Therapy Dog stories of ours and letters in his mailbag from other Therapy Dogs in the Club. Dogs do make a difference.

All in all, Milton and Milton's Magnificent Marilyn Monroe are not vegging on the couch but running with the winners and loving life.

WHO'S THE "BANDIT?"

By Steve Kalinoski

Tasha, a Siberian Husky, had a litter of three puppies in her youth. They were all given away. Maybe that precipitated her odd behavior later in life.

As Tasha got older, we acquired a Pit Bull Terrier puppy. Properly socialized in their early weeks, pit bulls, contrary to common belief, can be sweet, non-threatening dogs. She was. We called her Bandit. When Bandit was two years old, she had a litter of ten puppies. That's when the fun began.

At the opportune time, when Bandit was otherwise occupied, Tasha, now eight years old, would steal three of the puppies, and keep them hidden until Bandit found them. This happened daily – always the same three pups. Was she regressing to the time in her life when she had three pups of her own? Did she particularly like these three? Or was she jealous because Bandit had so many and she didn't have any? Whatever reason, she continued to steal, then hide the puppies, much to Bandit's bewilderment. Bandit would leave the others and frantically search for her missing babies.

The day after Thanksgiving, Tasha kidnapped the threesome again and hid them under a shed. Earlier, she had spotted a turkey carcass in my neighbor's trash. What a find! Being a good surrogate mother, feeding the babies was primary to her. She lifted the carcass out of the trash and carried it to the three little ones under the shed. When we found them and the evidence, she looked very pleased with herself.

All this may have been a constant annoyance to Bandit, but Tasha was never happier.

BENJAMIN BEAR-HEARTED

By Vicky Risko-Schaeffer

Our first two dogs were Rottweilers, a half-brother and sister born one year apart, named Ben and Gretchen Bear. As puppies they looked like Teddy Bears, hence their last name. I used to call Ben a benign dictator because, although he was definitely the Alpha dog, he put up with a lot of puppy terrorism from Gretchen. I think he was just so happy not to be alone anymore that no torture was too much

30

for him to bear. Of course, as she became older, the play became rougher on his part, but it was always play. They would snarl and growl, run at each other from across the yard at full speed, bang chests, tussle on the ground and then stop, go get a drink, and relax in the shade.

When Ben was three and Gretchen was two, my mother came to live with my husband, Paul, and me. My father, William, had died of A.L.S., a.k.a. Lou Gehrig's disease, and my mother, Margaret, could not live alone, since she had Alzheimer's disease. You have to understand that my mother had been afraid of dogs nearly all her life, since she had been bitten by a dog when she was very young. Now she was to live with two very large dogs that had the run of the house. At the time, she could speak only a little, and not really react to outside stimuli, as you or I might. And although I did not see any fear in her eyes, I am sure she was less than comfortable.

Ben decided immediately that Margaret was someone special, who needed his love, guidance and attention. Whenever Margaret was helped to walk to her recliner, or to the kitchen table, or to the stairs to go to bed, Ben was right there at her heels, making sure that she made it safely to her destination. Of course, if that happened to be the table for a meal, Ben and Gretchen took their places at either side of her chair, just in case their assistance in maintaining floor cleanliness was required. And while Margaret was still able to feed herself, it always was.

Once I asked my mother if she were afraid of the dogs, she answered simply "No." Then I asked her if she realized how much they loved her, especially Ben, and she answered, "Yes." For Mom, at that point, that was a speech, and it proved to me that she felt comfortable around them. This was made more obvious one day while I was at work, and our long-time nurses' aide, Cindi, was giving my mother lunch. As always, the dogs were on sentinel duty at my mother's sides. As Cindi watched, Mom held part of her ham sandwich down in front of Ben's large face, and said "Here, Here." Ben looked at Margaret, looked at the sandwich and back again, seemingly as astonished as Cindi was. Finally, Mom must have decided that Ben wasn't hungry, and she ate the sandwich herself. Cindi couldn't wait to call me at work and report this minor miracle.

This love that Ben felt for my mother lasted, sadly, only one year. One Sunday evening, almost one year to the day after my father's death, the nurse was leading Mom to the stairs for bedtime. Ben was at his customary place at her heels, when he suddenly groaned and fell over. I immediately called our veterinarian, while my husband checked Ben and performed CPR. Our doctor arrived fairly quickly, but by that time it was obvious that he was gone, at age four. One moment he was healthy and happy, and the next he had left us broken hearted. Our vet performed a necropsy on Ben, and told us that he had had an aneurysm near his right ventricle, probably since birth, and it had burst. He had died within two heartbeats.

Rottweilers are on that growing list of "bad dogs" banned in some municipalities and by some insurance companies as too dangerous. I agree that some breeds are better with children or other pets than other breeds, but no breed is inherently "bad." There is bad breeding and bad, even malicious, training that can result in badly behaved dogs with bad temperaments, no doubt about that. But branding a breed as bad is, well, bad and wrong. Our rotties were prime examples of good, loving dogs that wouldn't harm anyone. They proved, as especially Ben did, that they would love anyone we brought into our home. That being said, I must admit that I wouldn't have wanted to be a burglar breaking into our home!

LEMON PIE CAPER

By Rose Horrocks

TASTYKAKE lemon pie is one of my favorite things. I left one lying in the middle of the kitchen table, thinking that I would eat it after lunch. I left and ran my errands and when I came back my Poodle, Mitzi, did not meet me at the backdoor, as she usually did. I was concerned.

I began to hear this strange belching noise coming from the dining room. I peeked around the door. There was the TASTYKAKE package torn apart and Mitzi sitting belching loudly, one after another. She didn't get sick, she just belched the afternoon away and I was deprived of my lemon pie.

We both survived.

THE SAGA OF BENJY

By Jean S. Barto

Although Benjy, a thirteen-inch Beagle, has been gone one for 30 years, friends and neighbors still talk about his antics. There is one adjective that best describes Benjy, sweet. However, life with Ben was never dull.

Before he was a year old, he had been hit by a car, chewed to the bone by Bull Terrier (he never was a fighter), and caught upside down by a back paw entangled in a chicken wire fence, that had been designed to keep the little roamer in.

And then there was Spanky, a Dachshund, his best friend that lived across the street. They played daily, rolling around and chasing each other. One day, while mouthing each other, Ben's lower jaw caught in Spanky's collar. The harder he tried to free himself the more he choked Spanky. The screaming sounds they made brought everyone running. By that time, Spanky was bleeding from the mouth and Ben was frantic. We raced for heavy shears, cut the collar and freed both dogs. Spanky survived and Ben was chastened.

Benjy's housekeeping was not quite up to Martha's standards. Left home alone, Ben would upend a wastebasket right at the front door. Was he doing his chores or showing his displeasure that we had gone out?

A loaf of bread left on the kitchen counter was an open invitation when he was left alone. After eating enough for three sandwiches, he tidily would stash one slice behind each sofa cushion, saving enough to hide a slice under each bed pillow. What a surprise when you climbed into bed! Was he squirreling away enough for tomorrow, being Tessy Tidy or hiding the evidence? Who knows?

When he was about two, we moved to Pennsylvania and his legacy began anew. He was a smart little dog; learned to sit up, shake hands, bring in the paper, and roll over. One thing he never learned was to come when called (rather important). Being a scent hound, he would put his nose to the ground, tail high and off he'd go in true merry Beagle fashion. No matter how loudly you called, he feigned instant deafness.

Somehow his nose and appetite were tightly linked, and that caused some notable events. When we entertained, cocktail hour was his favorite. When he wasn't resting his sad little face on the coffee table, he would pick up his food bowl in his teeth and take it to each guest for a shrimp or cheese handout. He wasn't fussy. Who could resist?

Having the children gorge on Halloween candy was never a worry for me. No matter where the bags were hidden, Ben found then and enjoyed the loot, much to the kids' dismay.

The brownie fiasco was the eating feat that really made him famous in the neighborhood. My husband, then a food salesman, left a six-pound bag of dried brownie mix in an available spot. Never missing a food opportunity, Benjy devoured the whole thing. He swelled up like a spotted thirteen inch hippopotamus, sat in front of the heating vent and groaned. Any normal canine would have returned the repast on the oriental rug. Not Ben, he digested the whole thing. Linings of Dempsey Dumpsters couldn't match the lining of Ben's stomach.

He survived this dietary onslaught and topped it off many months later by going out garbage foraging on Christmas day. An X-ray showed he had swallowed five bottle caps. Time went by and he managed to pass them all. Ouch!

He won the prize with the next antic. One Saturday morning in late summer when all the neighbors were out mowing, weeding, and doing outside chores. Benjy pulled his Houdini and escaped. A short time later, he reappeared. All yard work stopped as the neighbors watched Ben trudging doggedly up the street. My husband raced to the door, calling, "Come here, quick." I flew to the door, opened it just as Benjy dropped his prize inside, a clucking, strutting chicken. Belying his voracious appetite, he had carried the chicken gently and safely home for our praise. Unfortunately, his gift was not only unappreciated, but was packed in the car and deposited over the fence of the nearest farm.

Ben lived to be almost 18. He was and still is deeply embedded in our hearts and became a furry legend in our community. Thirty years later, he still prompts many stories and laughs. A sweet, endearing, lovable clown – that was Benjy.

ADVENTURES OF MITZI AND CHERIE

By Rose Horrocks

One summer, George and I decided to go to Lake Placid for a week. George's sister and family agreed to dog sit our first Poodle, Mitzi. Their poodle, Cherie, was Mitzi's littermate, so it seemed like a happy arrangement.

The week was eventful, anything but peaceful for the caretakers. The stories of their antics that we heard on our return were frightening and amusing. Mitzi became a chicken chaser and had great fun seeing the results. Brother-in-law, Ed, was not too happy about that.

Then one day Mitzi and sister, Cherie, decided to take a hike down the mountain and wound up trotting along Route 100. Our patient dog sitters became alarmed when they couldn't be found. These were very specially bred dogs and could have easily been taken and sold. After several hours of concern, some good soul spotted them. She got Elaine and Ed's phone number from Cherie's name tag and called to let them know they had been found and were safe. We were very fortunate and grateful to get them back, and our dog sitters were happy to wave goodbye to Mitzi.

She wasn't invited back.

CHARLEY

By Anne Bower

Charley – now there's a name that warms my heart. I had the pleasure of having this Cairn Terrier for ten years. He went back and forth with me to Florida. The past five years because of airport security, he was searched. I'm sure Charley must have thought, while they were feeling his body, "Do I look like a terrorist?" However, he put up with it, all to be in Florida for the winter.

One winter we had a cottage on a nice Florida lake. How nice, I thought, there are palm trees on the lake's edge. I can tie Charley to one of those trees, give him a long leash and he can play at the water's edge. I no sooner got in the house when the phone started ringing, the people banging at the door, "Get that dog away from the lake, there are alligators in there!" What did I know? We don't have alligators in Philadelphia. I understand now, they love little dogs, too.

It was past lunchtime and Charley and I were at a strip mall. I looked in a local luncheonette. It was empty. Ah, a good spot for us. So, in we went. The fellow behind the counter was preoccupied when I ordered, so Charley and I just took a back table. About half way through my sandwich, the dog let out a bark. Oh hell! With that the manager's door flew open and he said, "Did you hear a bark?" I said nothing, just tried to look innocent. The manager returned to his office. Ah oh! Another bark. Now the manager knows for sure. Said he, "You cannot have a dog in here."

I was quick that day, "Would you believe he is a seeing-eye dog."

"Oh no," said quicker manager, "I saw you reading the wall menu."

"Come on, Charley, we don't need this place."

In Ireland and England, at least in the country pubs, dogs are welcomed. Most of the pub owners have their own dogs there. Perhaps someday we'll be as civilized as those pub owners.

Charley has gone to the happy pub in the sky – do I miss him, just every day.

JULIET, THE BEAGLE

By George Hilton

Growing up in the city did not allow for much opportunity to have a pet other than the periodical box turtle and the traditional chicks at Easter (which seem to disappear to the farm when they got too big).

I never understood why my father, having been born and raised on a farm, did not seem to want a dog for a pet. He always spoke fondly of the dogs that they had on the farm, so I knew that he liked them, which added to the mystery.

One day I asked him why we never got a dog and was surprised at the answer. He said that he felt that the city was not a natural place for a dog since they needed room to run, and he would not have a dog without enough space for it to be a dog. Now I clearly understood his respect and feelings for animal. Having come from a farm, to him, animals were not pets but partners in managing the farm.

My father retired and moved in with my sister and her family in the suburbs with a house that had about three quarters of an acre of land. She and her husband decided to get a dog for their children and into the picture entered Juliet, the Beagle. There are a number of stories involving her but these are the ones I liked the best.

I had married and moved into my own place, but had the opportunity to get to know Juliet during frequent visits. Juliet, at some point, seemed to forget that she was the family pet and decided that she was one of the children. Whenever the older boy, who was about two or three at the time, would walk across the yard holding his blanket and sucking his thumb, Juliet would make a mad dash at him and try to steal the blanket.

Whenever she could not make a clean steal, there would be a tug of war that resembled something straight from the *Peanuts* comics strip when Linus and Snoopy entered blanket combat. Eventually, one of the adults in the house would have to retrieve the blanket or part the two of them and chastise Juliet. This seemed to deter her for about two hours before the next attack. The target was too tempting for her to stay away.

The second story involves the flower beds around the yard. My father told me the story and then I got a chance to see it first hand. He had planted a border of various flowers around the perimeter of the yard which was enclosed by a small wire fence. These were off limits to the kids, including Juliet. Of course, there were the standard reprimands, whenever one of them went into the flower beds, unless there was a reason. The most common reason for going in was to retrieve a ball that would invariably go in during play.

Juliet made the connection that if the ball landed in the flower beds, she could go in and retrieve it without repercussions, if she asked permission. She would bark to get my father's attention, point out the ball and get the okay to go in and retrieve it. He would give her a hand signal and she would jump over the fence, get the ball and jump back out.

One day my father noticed that balls were going in the flower beds quite often, even when there were no kids around throwing them. He then discovered the reason when he caught Juliet red-pawed in the act. Whenever she wanted to enter the flower beds, she would take a ball in her mouth, toss it into the part of the beds that she wanted to enter, bark to get his attention and wait for permission to go get the ball. Needless to say, my father enjoyed her cleverness too much to ever stop her.

The third story involves me and a little family tradition that started on holidays. Being the youngest of the uncles in a good-sized family, whenever we all got together for an occasion, it became a mandatory event that I would be attacked and wrestled by all the children simultaneously. There were usually about eight nieces and nephews of varying ages, from two to ten, attacking me as I lay on the floor. The children had no plan, they would simply pile on Uncle George wherever they saw an open spot to attack.

During one of the attacks, as I was fending them off as best I could, I noticed that one of the "kids" who had landed on my head seemed to be very hairy. That was when I realized that I had acquired another niece and Juliet had jumped into the middle of the fray to get Uncle George. So from then on, I was attacked by nine nieces and nephews.

I am not certain that we could have ever made Juliet understand that she was not one of the children in the family.

DUMB AND DUMBER

By Gail Kelley

PETER TAKES A SWAN DIVE

Peter was a puppy mill, miniature Dachshund. He lived in a cage in a dank, dirt-floor cellar. I got him when he went sterile at the age of two and was no use to the breeders. They had never bothered to socialize Peter with people. Those who train seeing-eye dogs have learned that dogs need to be socialized when they are between six and sixteen weeks old or they will not understand people's behavior for the rest of their lives. Peter had clearly missed the boat.

He was not the Albert Einstein of the dog world. Everything confused him, not just people. Leaves falling from the trees terrorized him. He clung to me as his only protector in the world. When I took a shower he had to peak around the curtain to be sure I had not disappeared off the face of the earth. No matter how often he saw my friends and relatives, each time they visited it was a terrifying first.

I didn't realize how upset he was about strangers until my sister Karen visited. Peter saw her often, but apparently not often enough. I was soaking in a bubble bath and Peter was in his usual spot next to the tub. Karen walked in and sat down to chat. Peter did not react for several minutes. Suddenly, he leapt into the air and did a perfect swan dive into the tub and sank like a rock. I was so startled I dropped my book and began to laugh. When he failed to resurface, I fished him out of the bubbles. He looked like a worried, drowned rat. I wrapped him in a warm towel and held him until he fell asleep.

ABBIE TAKES OVER

Peter continued to be worried and dependent, finding it increasingly difficult to be alone. I decided to get him a companion. I answered an ad from a backyard breeder who was selling a two year old female. They said they were switching breeds so they were selling their Dachshunds. It quickly became evident that Abbie was sent out the door because she was a very dominant, poorly behaved little girl. Peter was horrified by her at first. That didn't matter to Abbie. She merely sat on Peter's head until he acknowledged her. Soon he was her slave. He adored her and she ran his life, stealing his food and depriving him of his toys.

If there were two bones, Abbie had them both. Once Peter took one of Abbie's bones and hid it in a room Abbie rarely visited. For a week, Peter chewed the bone when Abbie was outside. When she returned, he danced around her and teased her, something he never did. Eventually, she found the bone and Peter's moment in the sun was over. He never teased her again.

TRUMAN

Truman was a rescue dog who had been found starving in the streets and placed in the animal shelter's night drop. After a month in the shelter, a rescue organization saved him from the needle. When I got him he was a wreck, skin and bones and completely neurotic. He never sat still. He was particularly nervous at night. He sat and stared at me while I was sleeping. If I opened my eyes, he jumped off the bed, barked and ran in circles. After a month of sleepless nights, I was at the end of my rope. One night he had one dervish episode too many. I picked him up and locked him in a bear hug, talking softly to him until he calmed down. Finally, we both fell asleep. Eight hours later, I awoke to dog kisses and he was still locked in my arms.

That was the turning point. He was in love. I couldn't sit down without him sidling up to me and begging for a hug, the tighter the better. Adoring looks and contented sighs followed every hug. He stopped the frenetic circling and began to put on weight.

Years have gone by and Truman is now an old dog, but he has never stopped loving a hug. In the middle of the night he will crawl under my arm, give me a kiss, and put his head on my shoulder.

SUZY'S SECRET

By Camille J. Dawson

Once you own a Poodle, you may not be happy with any other breed, so go the words often heard in the dog world. Poodles; toy, miniature or standard sizes, are intelligent, loving and easy to train. They understand dozens of verbal commands and frequently know what you are going to do before you do it.

Suzy, my eight-pound Toy Poodle, was a daily joy. She was always affectionate, listening to our words, trying to please and be the center of attention. Take the day my Dad lost his wallet. He had been food shopping a few hours earlier. I called the super market for him and was told, "Sorry, no wallet was found."

Was it somewhere in the house? My Dad and I, with help from a neighbor, searched upstairs and down, under the furniture, the sofa and chairs, under cushions and pillows, in the closets and in the car, to no avail. Our nerves were frazzled. It was time to make the calls to cancel and replace his missing cards. Medicare was first on the list. I rang the number and was requesting a new card when.... At that moment, Suzy walked into our kitchen carrying the wallet in her mouth. She dropped it at Dad's feet. Wagging her tail, she looked up at him for a show of praise and a treat, of course. We were stunned, our mouths flew open. It was weird but what a big relief!

How did Suzy find the wallet when three humans could not? It was one more example of our unbelievably smart, devoted, almost perfect Poodle.

THE BEST EXCUSE EVER

By Tom Garvey

I hate parades. I hate the whole Army drill and ceremony thing. I hate marching, shining boots, badges and the overwhelming horseshit of it all. I was once a soldier. The jungle, with a gun and a rucksack, was where I felt comfortable. The Army Reserve Unit I served in for just over a year, after I came home and finished college, "laid on" a parade command formation. I thought there was no way anyone could get out of it. I was wrong.

Our Colonel, a loveable hardass, was a 'mustang,' a man promoted in the field from a young sergeant in Korea to 2nd Lieutenant, and through the years worked his way up in the Reserves to the rank of Colonel. He worked it well but the ornery 'sumbitch' loved a parade.

He stood before our formation one hot July morning and bellowed profanely that the parade the following day was important to him, and we would march precisely in razor sharp creased fatigues with spit shined, jump boots. The media would be there; we would be impressive. Attendance was mandatory. Death would not be an acceptable excuse.

We marched and drilled all day in miserable moist sweltering heat, a record high July day. I hate marching. I hate drill and ceremony. I hate parades.

We marched all afternoon. We marched well. We marched very well. It wasn't good enough. We marched some more. We looked good. We looked very good. It wasn't good enough. I'd jump out of an airplane at night into a swamp with blasting caps between my legs rather than march in a parade. We marched as one, every footfall to the exact beat of a single drummer, no maverick feet out there, and still as the sun set we stayed beyond normal duty hours to march some more. We marched and cursed until no one could tell anymore if we were in step or not. It was dark. We went home to come back in the morning and maybe practice some more. It wasn't a parade. It was a punishment.

I got home to the old Victorian house I'd lived in through college and limped up the stairs to the second floor. My door was open. In seven years, none of us ever closed, much less locked, our doors, unless we had "overnight company." I was coming home hours after I thought I'd be home, and the time I thought would be spent washing, drying, starching and pressing my fatigues and spit shining my one pair of jump boots, had been squandered on the parade field.

I walked down the hall to the open door at the far end. A throaty growl threatened me from the kitchen. I pushed the door open, "Harry, relax buddy, it's me!" The big black Lab with a purple bandana sat down, tail wagging. I took one of Studo's two last beers out of the refrigerator, popped the top and went in to sit on the corner of his bed.

Harry trotted along with me. I unlaced my boots and dropped them on the floor and covered them with my fatigue shirt and pants, and a pair of damp socks. I walked out of Studo's apartment, heading for the shower and took his last beer, with Harry's blessing. I popped the cap under the waterfall of shower water. I love drinking beer in the shower.

Later I met my friends at the Campus Casino. Everybody was there. I staggered home alone a little after four a.m. I came home alone because I knew I had to stay up all night and prepare my boots and uniform. I'd wash and dry my uniform in the basement and carefully press it, using almost a can of spray starch. My boots, I'd done them so many times over the past five years, I could spit shine them in my sleep. I'd be standing tall at the parade even if asleep on my feet.

There was no way out of the parade. I could hate it but I couldn't get out of it. At the top of the stairs, I stood outside my door weaving as I reached for the door knob. I didn't have to fish for keys as the door was closed, but not locked. I saw something I didn't recognize at first down the hall in front of Studo's closed door. I walked toward a pile of something, realizing it was my uniform, in a big damp sweaty ball, my boots on top. Walking back to my door with the pile in my arms, I somehow stuck my hand in the top of my boot. I looked at my hand. I couldn't comprehend what I was seeing. I stood outside my door confused. My hand had come out of my boot through where the toe should have been. The whole front of the boot, including the sole, was eaten away. Harry had an affinity for leather. Harry had eaten my boot! It was ruined forever, beyond repair. I went into my apartment and flopped on the bed laughing. I wouldn't be marching. I wouldn't be staying up to press my uniform. I didn't set the alarm.

A little after nine a.m., I woke up, dressed in civilian clothes. I took my boots with me. The parade was over by the time I arrived on the base. I passed a few friends who looked at me like I was a condemned man. Some turned and followed my car just to see the scene we all knew would not be pretty. A small crowd gathered behind me, as I pulled up by the curb on the company street. Fifty yards away marched the Colonel, flanked by a Captain on one side and a Major on the other. No one was smiling.

At 20 yards the colonel bellowed, "Stand where you are Lieutenant. Stand where you are!" The Colonel's voice was threatening, as he meant it to be, a tone that none of the men ever wanted to hear. I was on the side walk outside the car, the still wet boots cradled in my arms.

At 10 feet all three men stopped and the Colonel bellowed, as though he were across the parade grounds, "Account for yourself!"

I put my hand in my boot and came to ramrod straight attention. As my hand shot out of the ragged toe, I saluted the Colonel smartly through the boot, saying in a loud voice, "Sir! A dog ate my uniform!" The Colonel, looking like he was trying to eat his face, couldn't control himself. The Major lost it, the Captain looked uncomfortably bemused, as if he didn't know if he could laugh or not.

When the Colonel started shaking his head and laughing, I knew I was okay. There wasn't going to be a firing squad today, I'd come up with the perfect excuse. Harry was going to get a big bone for this one --- or maybe my other boot.

"BOGEY" – MY GIFT FROM GEORGE

By Carole Schoendorfer

My late husband, George, and I had always wanted a dog but felt that as long as we both worked that it wouldn't by fair to a pet. You don't bring an animal into your home and then ignore it or leave it alone too long. Then in April 1993, I was hospitalized again with Crohn's disease, and this time had 12 inches of my large intestine removed. I never worked again. With a chronic disease, I wanted to enjoy my life: have fun, go to lunch (more than one hour) with girlfriends, and play golf two or three days a week. Just truly enjoy life. This was also the perfect time to bring a dog into our home.

Late October 1993, I was in San Francisco visiting my sister. She was on the phone with my husband saying things like, "Yeh, okay, uh huh, yeh." What was that all about?

A dog had been abandoned on a Tuesday at the then Oak Terrace, now Talamore Golf Course/Country Club. We were members. The club called the Ambler Police department to report this dog. The police department said they had no missing dog report, but DO NOT put a found ad in the paper because animal labs answer those ads claiming found dogs and cats, and then use them for experiments.

The management at the club then called the Humane Society, who said they would pick up the dog, but because he was nothing special he would be destroyed in three days. The club management told them to forget it. We'll find him a home. For the next several days this dog slept in the bag room, got scraps from the kitchen and rode around the course in a golf cart with the general manager. Everyone loved this friendly dog with no tags.

Saturday, October 30, 1993, my late husband was playing golf with his best friend and it was pouring. After five holes they called it quits and went into the clubhouse. George heard all about the dog and when he saw him, it was love at first sight. We now owned this wonderful dog that was indeed special! The dog was named Bogey since he was abandoned at a golf course.

Bogey was the best! He was my dog during the day. When George came home from work, I ceased to exist. It was boy and his dog, 100 percent.

Then George died suddenly in March 1995. Bogey didn't know why I was crying all the time but he did his best to comfort me. He would jump on the couch and lick my face, licking away my tears. Another change happened. Bogey became alpha male and took over the role of protecting me.

At this time I traveled a lot. I would always drive because Bogey was big enough that he would have to fly as cargo. I wouldn't allow that. Bogey had been to more states than some people. He went from Maine to California several times with stops in several states. Bogey was the best traveling dog. He had the whole back seat on which to stretch out and sleep. I never had any fear traveling alone because Bogey wouldn't let anyone near the car or his mommy. His job was to protect me and he did … all the time.

Bogey and I lived in Santa Fe for six months. He accepted the two kittens I brought into our home. He and I and the cats moved to Tucson from Lower Gwynedd in 1998. He accepted happily every trip and every adventure we took. All the time he was my dog, my companion, my best friend and my protector.

Bogey was born with a heart murmur and the vets and I monitored him for years. Proper medicine, proper weight, proper diet. He was my life. His echocardiogram did not look good in August 2004. More medicine, more care.

October 5, 2004 I left for a hair appointment. When I got home, I knew it was his last day. I called the vet and immediately rushed him over. Bogey died in the car on the way. But he didn't die alone. He hung on, he waited until I got home to kiss me goodbye.

I miss my wonderful loving Bogey. I lost my two loves, husband and dog, to heart disease.

I am a better person for having had both of them add to my life.

Cats

"Cats are absolute individuals with their own ideas about everything, including the people they own."

John Dingman

CONFESSIONS OF THE CAT LADY OF WILLOW GROVE

By Kate Simon

I am a nice, normal housewife with a home, a husband and a job...I have five cats. I am certifiably insane.

SIMBA

I never intended to have cats. They, apparently, intended to have me. I have always been a dog person. Cat people sneered at me because I preferred the slobbering enthusiasm of my canine friends to the aloof distain of cats. I never minded picking up after my dog's walks but couldn't imagine keeping a litter box in my house.

Dog Person, definitely. That is until one frigid January night two years ago.

I am always dashing somewhere and on this particular night I was dashing into the market for a few groceries. The bitter January wind intensified my haste. I leaned into the wind and headed toward the crowded store. Half way to the entrance a high pitched sound reached me. There is nothing else in the world that sounds like a kitten, small and mewling and precious. I looked around to see. I was the only person in the parking lot save for the young boy collecting carts. I listened again and heard the sound of what was definitely a kitten in distress. The market was situated on a highway, nowhere near any residential areas. Some bastard had abandoned a kitten to the weather and the highway.

I moved my way around the parking lot until I located the sound coming from underneath an enormous Lincoln Continental. Getting on all fours, I spotted a dark shadow crouched near the enormous tire. The shadow cried and I moved for a better look. The light from a passing car hit the shadow, revealing a shivering calico kitten. I tried to reach under the car but fear of me was greater than fear of the cold. The ball of fur scrambled up inside the motor. Its meow echoed under the metal hood. I grabbed the box boy away from his carts.

"Don't let anyone start this car," I ordered.

"Why?"

"Because there's a kitten under the hood." Proof of my veracity came with a confirming meow.

Dashing into the grocery store (like I said, I'm always dashing), I purchased one easily opened container of cat food. I ran back to the car and laid flat on the asphalt, stretching as far under the car as I could. I held the open container under an opening and meowed at the kitten. The kitten meowed back. This exchange went on for several minutes.

"It's not coming out," I said to the box boy. "Go in and find out who owns this thing."

A few minutes later a gray haired man returned to his car/parade float to see a rather strange red head meowing at his grill.

"What are you doing?' he asked.

"You have a kitten in your engine."

"You're kidding."

"Pop the hood."

The man did as instructed and sitting on the carburetor was a crying calico kitten. I scooped it up before it could get further in the engine.

"Well, I'll be damned. How about that?" said the man.

"It wouldn't have been pretty if you'd started your car." I told the man in the hope he would have a little more faith in the next strange red head he encountered talking to his car.

The box boy helped me into my car. I slammed the door with a quick thank you as the kitten scampered free inside my car. As I sat at the traffic light, I tried to think what I was going to tell my husband. I also wondered how my dogs would react. Did I mention I have two dogs? Like I said, certifiable.

Montie is a Schipperke, bred to hunt rats and guard Belgian fishing boats. He had never expressed an interest in cats one way or the other. Lacey, our Bichon, had cat friends in the past, but never a tiny, terrified kitten. I had called my husband to warn him of my delay, but I failed to mention I was bringing the reason for the delay home with me. I thought quickly of the lines I could use to assure him I would just keep the kitten long enough to get it warm and find it a new home. After all, we were Dog People.

"What did you do?' he asked with the tone of a husband who was almost used to his wife's eccentricities.

"I couldn't let it freeze," I said, as I tried to hold the squirming kitten in my hands. Dogs were jumping and barking and the kitten was attempting to crawl vertically up my body.

"Well, you might as well put it down," he said with complaining tone, but he wasn't really complaining. He would have done the same thing and I knew it.

I set the kitten down and Lacey immediately pounced, not to attack but for the opportunity to groom a baby. She licked the kitten's head until it extricated itself from her tongue and dashed to the kitchen. A small hole in the back of a cabinet proved to be just big enough for the terrified kitten to hide in.

The dogs were barking, my husband was humphing like only an annoyed husband can, the kitten was hiding somewhere underneath my bread door…just another typical evening at home.

Advice, that's what I needed, or at the very least a litter box. I knocked on the door of the first neighbor I could think of who had a cat. I discovered all cat owners have extra litter boxes and keep a ready supply of litter. My neighbor explained the mechanics of the litter box, assuring me the kitten would be instantly trained. I had my doubts.

I came back to the house with my stash proudly tucked under my arm when my husband turned to me and announced, "You should probably run to the pet store and get Simba some toys, all we have are dog toys. And she can't live on tuna fish."

"Who's Simba?"

"She has to have a name," he replied.

I stood dumbfounded with the certain knowledge that my cat-free life was no more.

"Okay," I sighed, "you can keep her." He turned away to hide his little kid grin. (He will deny this to his dying day). I grabbed my keys and headed back to the car. I got to the door and shook a warning finger. "That litter box thing, that's all you, dude."

So began the learning process for two cat neophytes. We learned the hard way.

First, never shadow box with a kitten, you'll loose. I discovered this while entertaining Simba with my finger instead of the expensive feather toy. I still have the scar. A sub heading of this axiom; never sleep with your feet outside the sheets. Twitching toes are tempting targets. My husband discovered this when Simba split open his big toe like a sausage. Like I said…the hard way.

Second, kittens can fly. Well, not actually fly, but dish out some fishy smelling goop and a kitten can leap from a sitting position, four feet away, to right next to you on the kitchen counter in one move. I believe it should be aerodynamically impossible for a three-pound fur ball to do that. Engineers should study this, really.

Third, kittens are reincarnated mountain climbers. Simba was only four months old when she conquered Mount Bookcase. I discovered her achievement at 3:00 a.m., the discovery time for all great cat achievements, like broken pottery and hairballs, but I digress.

I was up like a shot at the sound of a heavy metal thud. I ran with motherly concern (Dad was still snoring away) to the location of the sound, the den next to our bedroom. Someone was hurt, I was sure of it. The dogs followed me to the den wagging sleepily, and I am sure cross to be wakened at such an hour. Simba. It had to be Simba. I was a terrible cat mom. Only a month and she was injured somewhere, I knew it.

"Simba. Simba, where are you, baby?"

I heard rustling and looked around, and then up...and up. On top of the seven foot high bookcase was a large artificial fern and a blank space where my brass candlesticks had been displayed. They were now at my feet. In the midst of the fern leaves were two golden eyes.

Which brings me to point Number Four; cats are interior designers. Simba claimed a hallway table as one of her many nests. She didn't mind the pictures of my parents. She could easily push them up against the wall...every freaking day. But the miniature ceramic pitcher had to go. This I discovered as my four-pound kitten carried the half-pound pitcher in her mouth down the stairs. Apparently, she felt it looked better in the living room.

We learned, slowly but surely. We got used to seeing an animal walk above, not below us. We got used to checking closets to see if anyone had taken up residence. We learned to accept the systematic destruction and eventual extinction of all houseplants. Simba staged a campaign against ferns that would have made Schwarzkopf proud.

Our education had just begun.

BABYCAT

Spring means flowers, sunshine and it means kittens. Heavily wooded, complete with babbling brook, our townhouse' backyard had always had its share of stray cats. They traveled from neighbor to neighbor, looking for a handout. I had never taken much notice of them before. Before, that is, we'd become cat people.

My husband called me to the back door one morning. "Look at that." He pointed to my neighbor's deck. Out from underneath the wooden slats popped a white cat with black spots I'd seen before. The cat had come and gone through my backyard for the three years we'd lived there.

"So?"

"Watch," Behind the cat, out popped a miniature version, all white with black spots on the head and tail.

"Ahh, a kitten." (Warning: Anything that inspired 'Ahh' from you is trying to move into your house).

There was only one kitten, only one survivor. Life outside, even with a babbling brook, is tough.

This was the beginning of the end of sanity.

We began to leave food and water at our back door. It was hot. She shouldn't have to feed her baby garden snakes. We told ourselves we had very good reasons.

Along with food, I gave them names. Being a writer and fancying myself exceedingly clever, I named them Mommycat and Babycat. We spent the next few months watching as Mommycat taught Babycat to catch slugs, hunt butterflies and wrestle well enough for the WWF.

We weren't the only ones watching. Simba stared out our French doors with great fascination at the activities. She looked like a little kid who wasn't allowed out to play. I felt sorry for Lacey, who, up until this point, had been Simba's dog mommy and the sole object of her affections. Lacey still groomed Simba on a regular basis and kicked her furry butt when she felt she needed it, but when Mommycat and Babycat's were outside, nothing could distract Simba. She made plaintive little meows in Babycat's direction and he came to the door. They did a dance back and forth, chasing each other the length of the screen. They chatted, making little meows and clicking noises, I'm sure discussing the merits of fresh slugs over canned salmon.

One day Simba looked at me with a face that said "Awww, Mom, can we keep him?" I was doomed.

Early that fall Mommycat decided Babycat was old enough to fend for himself. Instead of calling him back to their nest, she hissed at him. He came near her and she swatted him. He cried for her and she walked away. It may be nature but it broke my heart.

A conversation started harmlessly as I set canned whitefish outside my back door.

"It's starting to get cold," said my husband.

"Yeah, it is," I answered as Babycat came out of nowhere. "It's supposed to rain tonight, hard. I think I'll take the dog carrier and put it outside. Maybe Babycat will use it to hide out."

I wrapped a dog carrier in plastic, lined it with the dog's sheepskin blanket and dosed it with catnip spray, purchased in a futile effort to get Simba to use the expensive scratching post instead of the sofa. I opened the drapes the next morning to discover a white fur ball curled up inside the carrier. Babycat raised his head and stretched, pulling his long body out of the small box. I set down fresh water and a bowl of canned salmon.

Room Service.

The next few weeks Babycat developed a fondness for wet cat food and dry sleeping quarters. As I set out food I sat on the floor and slid my hand out the door. At first, Babycat shrank back. Then he began to sniff at my still hand. Slowly I was permitted a touch, a slight pet, and then triumphantly, a scratch behind the ear.

"I can't keep this box out here all winter," I said to my husband.

"No. We should just bring him in."

"You're probably right." I turned to hide my little kid grin.

The next Saturday morning I came out to find Babycat asleep in the crate. I reached out quickly and shut the door.

I now owned two cats.

I should have known something was up with Babycat when the vet was startled, he was five months old and nearly six pounds. Babycat grew, and grew, and grew. Yet there is not an ounce of fat on his now twenty pound frame. Babycat is just a big ass cat.

Our impulse with Babycat proved successful. Despite all the warnings I received about taking a wild born cat into my house, all was well. Simba and Babycat were inseparable. Simba became Babycat's substitute mom, grooming and showing him the ropes on indoor life. He even tolerated the occasional tongue bath from Lacey. Unlike Simba, who'd made short work of our slipcovers, Babycat used the scratching post.

Things couldn't have been going better; a sure sign things were about to get crazy.

MOMMYCAT

Winter was fast approaching and I was still feeding Mommycat. I discovered she had a fondness for anything bird. She started taking bits of chicken from my hand. After she'd had enough bird to fill her tummy I held my hand outside the door. The first time she brushed up against my fingers was a small victory. I was tempted to reach out but I resisted, allowing her to come to me. Eventually, I worked up to a ten-minute pet after every meal, scratching behind her ears and talking softly to her.

I put the dog crate back out, wrapped in plastic to protect it from the winter winds. Sheepskin blankets doused with catnip spray proved just as appealing to Mommycat as it had her son. I snapped a picture of Mommycat, warmly ensconced in the crate surrounded by high snowdrifts. This could not go on.

One morning, as we had our after breakfast pet, I reached my other hand out and snatched her into the kitchen. She hissed and spit when only moments before she was curling her head in my hand. With some inherent cat radar, she found the same small hole Simba had used her first night and slid her body through.

Hunger eventually won out and she came out of her hiding place to eat.

"Here you are, Mommycat," I cooed.

She looked at me with a fear that broke my heart. I would have to win her trust all over again.

"You're looking a little hefty, Mommycat."

It was Mid-February and a feral cat was fat. Things were going to get very crazy indeed.

It was the third morning Mommycat was with us. The night before the temperature had turned bitterly cold and it had begun snowing heavily. At breakfast I saw that

Mommycat had gone inside the covered litter box and wouldn't move.

"What's up with that?' I asked my husband.

"She'll be fine. Just give her some time. At least she's not outside in this weather," he replied as we both left for work.

Having a commute of only one block allows me to come home for lunch. That afternoon I came home, threw the mail on the kitchen table and froze. I heard several high-pitched meows. Mommycat was still in the litter box. In the box with her were five kittens.

I called my husband. "Now what do I do? She won't let me get near her and I have to get her out of the litter box. That can't be good for her and the kittens."

"Don't Penny and Steve have a vet that comes to the house?"

A quick trip to the neighbors and I put in an emergency call to their vet, Duke. I placed another call to my office that I would not be returning from lunch due to the sudden addition of five new members of my family. Margie didn't have to laugh that hard.

Duke arrived looking less like a duke than I expected. His slight, wiry frame proved beneficial to the treatment of Mommycat. He climbed over counters and moved himself into contorted positions to retrieve Mommycat. She hissed and spit as he held her tight, giving her shots and drawing blood. He literally sat on her while we waited for the result of the blood test for feline HIV to appear on the plastic stick. She was negative.

He let her go and she fled to the hole under the counter. Duke picked up each kitten and pronounced it in satisfactory condition. They were also pronounced all male. He placed them in the large dog crate I had prepared and I moved the crate in front of the hole. Mommycat instantly joined her babies.

"She looks like a good mother. They should be fine," said Duke.

Still in shock, I stared at the box of noisy, squirming fur, "At least they're not outside in this."

"They would have died," Duke said with terrifying certainty "Mommycat, too. She would have never survived the trauma of giving birth in this storm."

I looked back at the kittens, Mommycat staring at me warily. Timing really was everything for Mommycat and for me.

They say what a difference a day makes. They are a pain in the ass.

The next day one of the kittens started crying and wouldn't stop. Mommycat was ignoring the kitten that was off to the side of the crate, away from his siblings. I tried to get close, but Mommycat has a hissing, clawing force to be reckoned with.

I placed one more emergency call. "Duke, I don't know what to do."

"There is probably something wrong with the kitten. That's why she's ignoring it. You can try bottle feeding it."

A quick trip to the pet store and I returned with a miniature baby bottle and a supply of hope. My husband lifted the crate and tilted it just enough to make Mommycat leap out. As she sat in the corner, glaring at us, I placed the crate on the kitchen table and reached in. The plaintive meows had stopped.

I was too late.

Nature may be beautiful and wondrous, but sometimes it really sucks. My husband consoled me, telling me it was meant to be. There was probably a defect with the kitten. That didn't stop me from mourning a creature that died without a name.

MOOSE

Three days after the kittens were born; I had several nasty bits of my insides removed. Five days in the hospital meant daily visits and phone calls, not to check on me, but for me to check on the status of 'my babies'. My husband assured me that all was well. No, the dogs weren't tormenting them. Yes, Mommycat was eating. No, the kittens weren't crying too much.

The next month of my recovery was spent watching four little fur balls begin to explore their world, their world being my kitchen with the occasional glimpse into the far off universe, the living room.

The first kitten to peek his head out was the image of Babycat, shrunk down to less than one pound. The little boy sat boldly alone on the kitchen floor, looking up at me as some great cat mystery. He began springing around the kitchen with jerky bounces. He was first to eat solid food, or rather walk through the food bowl. He was first to discover the joys of a tongue bath from Lacey. He was also the first to discover that he could hide quite nicely underneath the refrigerator. This first little brave boy was christened Stormin' Norman

The second kitten to come out was the image of his father, who by this time we had identified as a stray from the neighborhood, we named Daddycat. (A writer, very clever). Just like his father, this kitten had a black hood of fur on his head and more black on his body and tail. A visiting neighbor said he reminded her of a Toby, so Toby it was.

The third kitten to explore was a carbon copy of his mother, MiniMe.

The last little kitten didn't so much bound out of the crate as he did waddle. Rounder, fluffier and twice the size of his short hair brothers, I took one look at him and said "Lord, what a Moose!" The name stuck.

As soon as I could stand, I grabbed my camera and snapped pictures. The kittens and the havoc they wrought became a constant source of amusement and diversion. It's hard to think of your stitches when a few ounces of fluff decides to crawl under your blanket and go to sleep.

Mommycat did a good job taking care of her babies, but was forever licking the dog spit off her kittens. The moment the kittens began to wander, Lacey took them to be hers. Mommycat was constantly retrieving her babies from their dog mommy and carrying them back to her nest. Montie remained aloof, distaining anything that diverted my attention from what was truly important, namely him.

The topic of new homes came up at six weeks.

"We have to start looking," said my husband.

"I know," I sighed.

"We can't keep them."

"I know," I repeated.

I found homes for three of the kittens. The new owners were people who promised to never de-claw and to return them to me, not a shelter, if they couldn't keep them. I didn't spend enough money on them to have paid for a top of the line computer system, only to have them wind up in a shelter. We agreed to let them go at twelve weeks.

Three down, one to go.

My husband called me at my office. "You really want to keep Moose, don't you?"

"A-huh," I muttered, knowing what he was doing.

"Well, I suppose there's not much difference between three cats and four cats."

I squealed into the phone.

MISSY

Memorial Day weekend. Everything was calm, or as calm as it can be with two dogs and four cats in your house. Babycat and Simba had taken an interest in Moose, chasing him around the house and showing him the ropes of kittenhood. Mommycat was enjoying a post partum rest. All was right with the world. (You'd think I would have figured this out by now).

"Meow."

We were sitting at the table enjoying dinner and ignoring the critters at our feet, begging for food.

"Meow."

I looked around. It didn't sound like any of our cats. Each had a distinctive 'voice' ranging from pathetic whining to demanding. I glanced at the back door. Sitting on the top step was a gray and black striped cat with the most amazing green eyes I'd ever seen.

"Meow."

"You can't live here," I shouted. "No vacancy. No way, Jose." My maternal instinct seemed to be on hold.

"Give him something," said my husband. "He looks hungry."

I set out a bowl of cat food laced with bits of our meatloaf dinner and a bowl of water. The cat sank its head into the bowl and devoured the entire meal. Hungry didn't cover it. The ridges of its spine and ribs were clearly visible. The tail looked like a fur stick someone had attached to the body. This cat was starving.

The wrapped crate went back outside along with the accompanying room service. But I was determined this one was not coming in. I thought I'd feed it enough to get its strength back while I looked for its owners.

Day after day the cat sat at the door quietly staring at me. "Come on. Who are you kidding? You know you're going to let me in. Do it already and get it over with. Otherwise I will sit on your back step and make you feel guilty forever."

On the seventh day, I finally agreed with the cat. I closed the door on the crate while it was asleep and took it straight to the vet. After a quick check the vet pronounced my new madness healthy, but hungry. Approximately eight years old, the cat weighed only six pounds. The cat had been de-clawed in the front, which would have made catching prey more difficult. And it was a she.

"She has probably been neutered. They may have done it when she was de-clawed, but with scars this old it's hard to tell without opening her up," said the vet.

"Great. I guess I'll have to see if she goes into heat." Just what I needed.

What our new addition needed was a little discipline. Fussing with her housemates, hiding in closets, sleeping on my head, she had to assimilate.

"I don't think so, Miss," became a well-worn expression in my house. "Get over yourself," I cautioned after a run in with Mommycat. "You live in a big family now." Think 'The Walton's' with fur.

For a time I allowed her to go in and out. She always returned and it was one less cat underfoot. That is until my neighbor told me that my cat was running into everyone's house. It seemed like she took any open door as an invitation. Some of my neighbors didn't take kindly to it.

Imagine that.

She was confined to the house. Each time she made a dash for the door I said "What do you think you're doing, Miss?" in that tone. I sounded just like my mother

Missy had joined the family.

TERRITORIES, DÉTENTE AND THE WORST SMELL ON THE PLANET

Each cat has his or her own unique personality. Blending them has not been easy. Simba is an adventurer, quick to hunt the errant housefly or the piece of chicken that just happens to be on your fork. Babycat, for all his size, is a shy love bug. He climbs on the bed in the night, nudging me with his head to be petted. Mommycat is my personal triumph. Skittish to the point of terror upon her arrival, she now comes when I call her for head scratches and lunchmeat. She has a thing for lunchmeat. It helped her bond with my husband, who has a similar obsession. Moose is still a kitten at a year and a half. He adores television. We bought him the movie "Ice Age" for Christmas. (Yes. We really did). Whenever we can't find him we put the movie on. As soon as he hears the opening cartoon, he flies into the living room and perches directly in front of the screen. Missy is my South Philly girl. Never one to start a fight, she is more than ready to finish it. The girl kicks fur.

Shortly after Missy joined us, the 'troubles' began. Each cat tried to carve out his or piece of territory in my eleven hundred square foot home. Missy decided the area on top of the dryer near the cat food was hers. We were introduced to spraying.

The wall was scrubbed down with enzyme cleaner and Missy was carefully watched. No sooner did we get her under control than Babycat started. As a tomcat it was to be expected, despite the fact that he was neutered. Babycat tried to identify everything in the kitchen at waist high level as belonging to him. He marked each corner of my kitchen counter, which I faithfully scrubbed and sterilized, and he, just as faithfully, re-marked. Babycat had a few surprises for me.

One evening after a long day at work I decided to cook, a remarkable event in itself. I threw the ingredients for stroganoff in the skillet and began to cook.

"What is that?" I asked no one in particular.

My nose twitched. Was the meat bad?

My eyes watered. It didn't smell like bad meat.

My nostrils began to burn. "What the hell is it?"

I pulled the skillet off the flame and turned off the stove. As I examined its contents, I glanced at my dark yellow range top. What had apparently been a puddle was now a crystallized spot between the burners.

I had discovered the worst smell in the world. It's not cat pee. It's HOT cat pee.

I did what any sensible person would do. I laughed my ass off.

The problem continued with increasing frustration.

"The book says he's stressed," I told my husband.

"What has he got to be stressed about?" he shouted. "He has all the food he wants, playmates and a queen size bed to sleep in."

After a call to a local rescue service for advice, I added a fourth litter box and bought an expensive bottle of spray that alleged to 'calm' my stressed out cat. Much to my surprise and relief, diligent cleaning of the boxes and re-spraying Babycat's favorite spots every couple of weeks reduced the problem from a constant frustration to a rare event.

Within a few months each cat had identified his or her favorite areas of the house. Mommycat rules the kitchen. Missy has possession of all heating vents. Moose loves the top of the china closet. Simba, who never met a meal she didn't like, claimed rights to the dining table. Babycat, well, when you weigh more than the dogs, you can sleep wherever you please. There are still the occasional skirmishes, but no one walks away broken and bleeding.

Détente has been achieved.

MONTIE AND LACEY (in the interest of equal time)

Why do I do it? I get asked that a lot. Two and half years after that night in the freezing parking lot, four thousand cans of cat food and one thousand pounds of cat litter later, I ask myself why.

One night, I got my answer.

All the animals, dogs and cats, have 'Mommy and Me' time. Mommycat is first thing in the morning while I drink my tea. Moose is post-tea, before shower. Each animal has a few minutes in my day when I pay attention only to them. Simba is 11:00 p.m., as I've settled into bed. She jumps up on my stomach and does 'the kitten dance.' Kittens knead their mother's stomach to stimulate milk. Cats continue the habit as a source of comfort. Simba finished her dance; carefully thank heavens, since I don't believe in declawing. After two circles of my waistline and she curled up on my tummy. I scratched behind her ear and under her chin as she purred. She rested her head on my stomach and dozed.

I had my answer. Two years before I'd found a tiny, half frozen kitten on a carburetor. Now, here she was, Garfieldesque, and sound asleep on top of me. I had made a life for that frightened little kitten. I made a life for all of them. I never intended for any of this or any of them to occupy my life so completely. But that night I came to understand what I did was important. Maybe it's only important to me; it's definitely important to them, but important just the same.

They are well fed, healthy, and content enough to fall asleep on my stomach.

All is well…

HOME FOR THE HOLIDAYS

By Pam Serra

When we lived in Erdenheim, Pennsylvania, we cared for a mother barn cat and her litter. Shortly after the arrival of the litter, we moved to another house in Wyncote, Pennsylvania, about five miles from Erdenheim. The mother cat and three of her offspring came with us. The mom had never been to the new house before and after her arrival, we kept her and the three little ones inside, thinking they might get lost in an unfamiliar area.

A week after the move, mom slipped out somehow with one of her kittens and they disappeared. Weeks went by – no sign of the vagabonds. One morning two and one half months later and, incidentally, the night before Christmas, I opened the back door and there they were, the mother cat and her little one. They came in, reconnected with the other kittens and spent the holiday season with us.

Shortly after the holidays, they disappeared again, never to return. We always wondered where they went right after our move, and how did they find our house at Christmas, when they had never been outside this house before. And most of all, why did they come back for a visit? We'll never know.

HOW ABOUT A THERAPIST

By Leah Heise

Caesar, a puffy Persian cat, has traveled a bumpy road in his two and a half years. When his owner, an elderly woman, died, Caesar and his housemate, a silver tabby, named Chase, were left homeless. My roommate and I rescued them and the adjustment period for Caesar and Chase started.

We loved them instantly, but transition is slow and not an easy thing for felines. Gradually the mismatched pair settled in. They slept curled up together most of the day. However, Caesar's wariness made him slow to warm up to me, but in a few months we bonded. He became a happy cat and slept at the end of my bed at night.

He still shunned brushing, a rather important ritual for Persians. Six months went by but Caesar still ran from the brush. His fur grew more matted. In desperation, I took him to a groomer to be unknotted. The suggestion was "shaving." So he was shaved to the skin except for fluffy ankle bracelets and his "I'm prettier than you are," kind of face. What a shock when I saw him! He looked like a French poodle's weird feline cousin. Even Chase eyed him suspiciously and wouldn't cuddle up for their afternoon nap.

The next day, I noticed an irregularity in his breathing. He was wheezing. Off to the vet we went. After an examination and Xray, the vet stated Caesar has fluid in his lungs and probably had cardiomyopathy, a disease common among Persians. He added that this would shorten his life to a few months or maybe just a few years. I was devastated. I had grown to love the little fur ball. The vet drained his lungs and I took a more comfortable Caesar home. However, before leaving the vet suggested having an animal cardiologist examine him.

After a few days of intensive worry, we visited the cardiologist. She found a mitro valve problem (heart murmur) but concluded he did not have the life shortening condition, heretofore suggested, of cardiomyopathy. He was not doomed to a premature demise, but would live a normal life. Hallelujah! She summarized that the wheezing had resulted from the trauma of being shaved. He was embarrassed and had a panic attack. Two hundred and fifty dollars later, her advice was, "Don't ever shave Caesar."

JASPER

By Lois Troster

The night is frigid and a big Tabby cat climbs the fence to look for his evening bowl of milk. It's there, and also the woman holding the saucer for him. He coughs and shakes. His throat is sore, but the milk is warm and delicious. Suddenly, the woman's arms are lifting him into the house across the window sill. There's another cat inside staring him down. That's good, he thinks, they like cats. He doesn't struggle because he knows he'll be as sick as the others, all feral cats huddled in a lean-to in the snow, needing human help. He's the biggest, 30 pounds, with gorgeous eyes, and only he knows the routine of the milk.

Suddenly he's terrified – riding in a car. Is she taking him to the pound or dumping him out on the road, never to find his way back to the shelter? Soon he's in another building with a man in white, all bright lights. She's telling the man that his name is Jasper and he's an Abyssinian Cuckoo cat. The man comments that he's not familiar with the breed, but the cat is sick so he'll help. I'll call tomorrow, she says to the man. He feels warm and safe and before long he goes to sleep. He now knows he is a very rare Abyssinian cuckoo cat and his name is Jasper!

Jasper lived to an old age. He liked to sit inside the fence he had climbed over every night many years before, but he never climbed over it again.

Note: The title Abyssinian Cuckoo cat lasted his whole life. My mother loved him and was afraid the vet would not take extra care with him if he knew Jasper was a common alley cat, so she quickly made up the breed name many years before and fooled the vet.

LOVE WINS

By Jean S. Barto

"There's BZ impatiently knocking at the window again," my husband would say as we sat watching TV in our second floor family room. He would go to the window, open it and in would march our athletic, striped tabby cat, who would be clearly annoyed that he had to wait 30 seconds for his knock to be answered.

BZ would jump up on a first floor window sill, leap from there to the small roof over our front door, then up onto a second floor TV room window sill, and scratch the window to be let in.

BZ was not only athletic but adventurous, curious and strong minded, too. One adventure took him to elementary school, not to enroll, but just for the ride. One morning a neighbor, a fourth grade teacher, hopped in her car to go to school. Remembering something she needed she ran back into the house, leaving the car door open. Bad mistake. As she approached her school, one half hour away from home, she felt a presence in the car. It was unsettling but she waited until she reached the school parking lot. She opened the door, reached in the back seat for her bag and saw BZ nestled on the back seat, obviously having enjoyed the ride.

Not happy about this, my neighbor threw her bag back in the car, thrust the car in gear and raced home to let the little stowaway out. I'm sure Judy ranked high on BZ's list of favorite people after such a lovely ride, however, BZ remained close to the bottom of Judy's list.

We loved this interesting critter. One morning when he was just five years old, he didn't bounce out of his bed like he usually did looking for his morning repast. We called him, then coaxed him but he didn't move. We lifted him out of bed and he could barely walk.

Next, we made a flying trip to the vet. After a thorough examination, he was diagnosed as having a virus that affected his central nervous system. The recommendation was to leave him for observation. We demurred. This is why.

Our previous cat, Ethel, a shy, sweet tabby, one time shocked and worried us. We hadn't seen her for two days, an unusual occurrence for her. Finally she made it home, tail totally limp and dragging. She either had fallen or someone had hit her with a shovel. Off to the vet's we went. The recommendation was to leave her for observation, which seemed like the right thing to do. We kept checking, we knew they would give her good care, but five days later the call came that she had died. We always wondered if her injury caused her death or had she felt abandoned by us, since she had never been away from home before, or a combination of both.

This brings me to a continuation of the BZ story. We refused to leave BZ at the vet's, although we knew they would give him excellent care, but the one overriding issue was abandonment. So, we opted to bring him in every two days for examination, hydration and injections. We were given pills for him and a high calorie paste to rub on his gums for nutrition. Being as sick as he was, administering the pills was not a problem.

It was several days before Labor Day weekend when all this started which didn't phase the vet. He said he would be there for us all weekend and he was.

My husband and I took turns holding BZ and nurturing him for the whole weekend. We kept his bed near us at night and handed him back and forth during the day. He could still barely walk. Labor Day arrived, I was in the kitchen. BZ's bed had been placed near the back door. I saw him get up, something he could not do before, go to the backdoor and step down the three-inch step. I yelled to my husband. Our care, combined with the vet's, had worked. He was starting to move. It looked like he was on the way to recovery. We clung to each other and cried. Each day he got stronger and after a couple of weeks, he was his old self.

BZ lived nine more happy, healthy years, continuing to enter the house through the second floor window when we were in the family room. What strong medicine love can be!

MR. PIDDLE
By Lyman Hanson

Our cat, Mr. Piddle, so named as a kitten for obvious reasons, regularly traveled back and forth with us to our vacation home at the shore. He never was a very happy traveler and would complain vociferously during most of the journey. And yes, there would occasionally be accidents in the cat carrier. These would sometimes require a hasty roadside stop for clean up.

The most notorious of these incidents occurred not more that a 100 yards from our front door. We had just acquired a snazzy new station wagon, our first car with air conditioning. On this particular trip it was necessary to take two cars, as I had to be back on the job after a couple of days, while the family planned to spend the week. I expected that most of the kids and Mr. Piddle would drive down in air-conditioned splendor, while I would have at least one passenger to keep me company. Alas, this was not to be. It was a very hot day and everyone opted for the A.C. I must admit that I was somewhat put out that I would be traveling alone, but I got my revenge. I rather enviously watched the car drive down the lane, when to my astonishment the car suddenly came to a screeching halt, all doors flew open and there was a mass evacuation of wife and kids.

It seems all of the excitement was too much for Mr. Piddle and he had a very odoriferous accident in the back of the car. The clean up was unpleasant, but, needless to say, I had plenty of volunteers to ride with me (not including Mr. Piddle).

MY CAT, PUNKIN

By Mercy Cunningham

At the barn where my daughter, Janyse, boarded her horse, there were five kittens. One day we decided to help ourselves to the most beautiful one. He was a long haired, orange colored cat, whom we named "Punkin." He was a delight, and reigned as king over the entire household, even over our Doberman.

Ten years later, my baby grandson and his mother came to live with us for a short time. Punkin objected strongly to this invasion. His reign had been supreme and now was threatened. He moved out.

He went to live with my neighbor, Ruth, who lived two doors away and had just lost her cat. He had a long and happy life with Ruth, as the ruling monarch. He visited us daily, just to keep an eye on things, but never came back to live. We still miss him.

NIKKI SAM

By Jane Walker, a cat lover

Nikki Sam and all her 'necessaries' were brought to me by her former owner, who had prayed for a new caretaker. Nikki was then 11 years of age, now 15. She is a female cat formerly named Samantha. Our former cat was named Nikki, hence the name Nikki Sam.

After she arrived, I couldn't find her for two weeks. She ate food I put out for her, drank water from her bowl and used the litter box but I never saw her. Who knows when the little phantom did all this? My neighbor (also a cat lover) finally found her hiding under my granddaughter's bed, and coaxed her out.

Now, she grooms herself everyday and is a grand 'live-in' friend. We are the best of friends, except when the cat carrier comes out and I ask her to go 'bye-bye' for her yearly visit to the vet for her exam and shots.

Nikki Sam is an indoor cat, who loves watching the birds, squirrels and bunnies out of the windows. A visitor called her a Russian blue. I call her an all-American gray and pink.

SHE'S A KEEPER

By Natalie Weiss

The soft meowing was barely audible at first, but as the minutes ticked on the cries became louder and more insistent. Being one who could never stand to hear a baby, of any kind, cry, Sara went to the door to see who the little whiner was. She opened the door and was peering around when gray stripes streaked by her into the house.

The door had hardly closed when the frantic exploration started. Every plant, sofa, table leg and kitchen corner was sniffed. The first floor feline examination took roughly 20 seconds.

Noticing no collar or tag, Sara wondered from where the stranger had come, and started to coax her soothingly to come to her. The little streak had other things in mind. Finding the stairs, she whooshed up to the second floor. Sara expected her to reappear in another 20 seconds after the second floor inspection was complete, judging by the cursory exam of the first floor. Soon the seconds became minutes and no sign of the furry detective. Prompted by curiosity, Sara went upstairs, scanned the bedrooms, peered under the beds and in any open closet but to no avail. As she passed the bathroom, Sara spotted the stranger, perched in a ladylike manner on the open toilet seat looking peaceful and immensely pleased with herself. She daintily descended and calmly walked past Sara like a model down a runway. Evidence pointed to usage of the facility.

Sara concluded the unrelenting meowing earlier indicated that the striped lady had been standing at the door with her legs crossed for a long time. Sara thought if no owner is found, she's definitely a keeper.

THE BRIDGE THAT CALI BUILT

By Jane Tamaccio

When I met Mrs. Cole in 1965, she had just begun her search for a music teacher in an effort to hopefully bring her daughter, Mary, out more into the world. No one had been successful in teaching Mary. She was mostly in her own world. It had not been possible to keep her in the "here and now." All efforts up to that point had been fruitless, because Mary had trouble relating to people and was afraid of any new experience. When Mary had been in treatment for some time, her mother happened upon the word "autistic" which seemed to describe her daughter's condition. Those with this mysterious illness have not learned to interact and give emotion back. Mary could not separate or function without her mother's presence, and she had no speech in those days.

The only thing that attracted Mary was music, but she was seriously emotionally disturbed. How could I help this child through music? Although I had been a piano teacher for more than 25 years, I had no former experience with a child who exhibited significant impairment, but in order to establish a relationship I would be led by Mary. We needed to create a dialogue. She needed to accept me, to feel safe and secure and draw me into her orbit. Then we would go to the piano. We would try to get a rhythm pattern started – she would strike a key twice – I would do the same, thereby producing a communication system. She was too threatened to relate to a human being, but not with an inanimate object. She and the piano responded to one another. I learned that you don't mold the child, you respond to cues – a mutual cuing. Mary opened vistas for me that I didn't know existed.

Mary's response to my calico Persian cat played a vital part in the course of her lessons. "Cali" would get up on the piano bench and sit along side of us. He would curl up on my lap and we would laugh and Mary started to speak, mostly about Cali's antics. I would say things like, "He thinks you came to see him. He doesn't realize that you came for a piano lesson. Look at him! Now he's sitting on your feet. Cali is getting up to sit on your book case. No matter what you are doing, he has to be present." Mary never thought of the cat as an intruder. Cali was merely acknowledging the presence of another human being. The cat noticed and responded. It helped to relax Mary as she watched his actions which were a response to her attention. (Animals do these things instinctively). After that exchange, Mary began to broaden her acceptance of other students.

To this day, my present cats have a meaningful role in my relationship with students helping me to create a bridge to them, as it did with Mary. The children can invest some of their feelings and discharge them on the cat. It's a method of allowing them to do that when they cannot perhaps feel free to discharge and invest feelings openly onto people. Previous to Mary, I had never conceptualized the possibilities that I could use my cat to help somebody, but Mary drew attention to his importance.

After more than 30 years, and following the death of her mother, Mary's sister arranged for us to have a meeting. When Mary came to the house, she had complete recollection of all objects, furniture, etc. Most of all she was immediately drawn to my watercolor painting of Cali.

So, we must always begin where the child is. A relationship must be established before goals can be achieved. The "living relationship" provides the child with an atmosphere in which he or she can recognize and accept shortcomings and capabilities. Cali was instrumental in connecting me to Mary and establishing that living relationship which is the essential element.

There are many things we can use to help a struggling child. We can't if we tend to think in mechanical terms. Many of my students love to groom and play with my cats when waiting for their piano lesson. Also, my cats respond to the piano music. It gets their attention and they enjoy being included. I have learned from my cats the value of their unrelenting devotion and acceptance of us as we are, as well as their value in our personal interactions.

THE CHRISTMAS ANGEL

By Beth Erdman Bauer

One October day, Dusty did not come home. Dusty, a 15 year old cat, was almost joined at the hip to my mom. Mom had severe arthritis and dearly loved this little snuggler. The feeling was definitely mutual, so when Dusty failed to return home, it was unbelievable. He always seemed to love his quiet, comfortable life in Laverock, Pennsylvania. Days passed, no sign of Dusty. What happened to him? All sorts of ideas surfaced, none happy.

We hunted, we posted pictures, sent out flyers, alerted all the neighbors. Weeks went by and then months. In response to the flyers, the "We saw your cat," phone calls started coming in. They became endless, but none reported a sighting that fit the Dusty profile.

Christmas Day arrived. He had been gone almost three months. It was early morning and we had all gathered in pajamas to exchange our gifts. The phone rang. I answered. A voice said, "I found your cat."

My response was snippy. After the dozens of bogus calls we had had, I figured my mom did not need one more false alarm especially on Christmas morning. A woman's voice said, "I really think it is your cat."

"Oh," I responded tersely, "What makes you think so?"

"Well, there's a cat outside with a pack of strays that I feed daily, and he has a collar on, which is unusual. Your phone number and the name Dusty is on the tag."

"That's him," I screamed excitedly. "You've found Dusty. Can you get him in? Where do you live? We'll be right over." The words tumbled out. My father was already putting his raincoat on over his pajamas.

"I live in Lynnewood Gardens," she added, (which is about three miles away). "I think I can lure him in with a can of tuna fish."

We ran out the door, while mom waited anxiously. The ride seemed two days long. Soon we were home with the little wanderer. My mom was ecstatic. This was our best Christmas present ever.

What had happened to Dusty during his hiatus from home? How did he find this pack of feral felines? Why did they accept this pampered, domesticated cat? Did he wander away, get confused and forget how to find home? We wondered if the pack sensed his age and possibly a touch of senility that impaired his ability to find his way, and took him in to care for him. We'll never know, but will always be grateful to his rescuer.

The woman who found Dusty, this kind animal lover, and my parents always kept in touch with each other after that. They exchanged Christmas cards and phone calls for years. She was our Christmas angel.

THE CONCERT

By Lois Troster

Many years ago when the summer home of the Philadelphia Orchestra was Robin Hood Dell, my mother and I were privileged to attend rehearsals. On cool summer mornings, sitting in the audience and hearing such world famous artists, we both had soul-satisfying emotions. Just watching, hearing the beautiful music and being allowed to view behind the scenes was a wonderful experience. World renowned conductors performed and artists from all over the world rehearsed and gave us both aesthetic pleasure.

We were befriended by one of the violinists. He spent his breaks talking to us, telling us all about his young son, who had just been accepted into the Curtis Institute of Music.

After the new season of the orchestra began, we watched our friend play on the Academy of Music stage, a change from the informality of the Dell.

One winter night our orchestra friend called and asked if he could stop by and visit. In moments we were enjoying a private concert in our living room by a world renowned violinist. It was surreal. Our two beautiful Persian cats hearing the music slipped down the stairs and sat under a chair, paws crossed, ears twitching. They never moved. They were fascinated by the sound. We never disclosed to the violinist that, in addition to the audience of three humans, there were two fur persons listening intently to the fabulous sound of a violin played by a member of the world famous Philadelphia Orchestra.

THE "EYES" HAVE IT

By Mary Parker

My cousin, Peg, always had a pet cat. The one I remember most vividly was a very large, all white male, named Joe. The pictures of him in her photo album attest to his being pampered, especially on holidays, when he was always dressed up in something special for the occasion.

When taken for rides, it didn't matter to Peg if his white hair shed, because when ordering her car she specified all white upholstery.

No doubt many people have white pet cats, so what makes this story different? Peg was born with one brown eye and the other eye green and so was Joe. It just seems they were meant for each other.

THE "PURRFECT" ANIMAL

By Ellen James Repeta
Age: eleven

"Hello, I am Mittens. I am a brown, patched tabby cat. I live in a huge house. I have two playmates, Noodles and Biscuit, both dogs. Sometimes I pretend I'm a dog and chase them. When I am bored I play with my owner, Elle. When I am tired I lay on a couch near a window. I am not allowed outside but I love to get out anyway. What I loved best was when I was adopted from the shelter. Here is where my story began."

ELLE'S STORY

The 'purrfect' animal is a cat. In this case I am talking about a cat named Mittens. She is so funny and cute. She has done many things but the first time I met her was one of the funniest times of my life. Here is what happened.

One day we lost our cat so my mom and dad said that we could get a kitten. So we looked everywhere. Then my mom said, "Let's go to the Lehigh Valley Shelter."

When we went there, there were millions of kittens, cats, puppies and dogs. There was a separate room for each. We wanted a small cat so we looked in the cages with the small kittens. I wanted a really playful kitty so I looked carefully. All of a sudden I saw a kitten chasing her tail, round and round. I told my mom I wanted that kitten. We asked the lady at the counter if that kitten was taken and she wasn't. It took one whole day until I could pick her up. It took so long because they had to do some tests and make sure everything was 'purrfect'. It was long for me but definitely worth the wait. That was the first time I met Mittens. She's a lot of work but well worth it.

Mittens added, "I agree."

WEBSTER, AN INTUITIVE CAT

By Lois Troster

Intuition. Most animals possess it, especially cats. They can sense danger with ears and whiskers. Remember, animals ran to higher ground before humans had any inkling of the Tsunami.

This is the story of Webster, a sick, hungry kitten whose sense or intuition saved his life and future. Picture a cold, wet spring day, a vacant house and a gray kitten, lost, afraid and hungry, crawling out of the bushes, just as a family gone for six months, arrives for vacation. The kitten approaches them, wondering if they will ignore him or hurt him. Luckily, he seems to know they like cats, and he cries and purrs as they pick him up. Weeks later, Webster was healthy and flying back to California. A nice happy ending!

But let's examine the elements here a little further. If Webster had wandered into that yard one week, one day or one hour earlier, they would not have been there. Had he wandered to the right or left, he would have been on a highway. And had he gone to another house, perhaps the people there weren't cat lovers. Circumstances, luck, good choices or intuition, whatever, the kitten had, gave him the luxury life of a California cat!

Cats are intuitive. They can smell food faraway, sense predators, and find someone to love them. Webster's story proves it!

WELCOME TO THE CATNIP BAR
By Lois Troster

Snowball, an elegant white Persian cat with stunning blue eyes and a plume tail, was allowed a daily trip outside because he lived in an isolated area. One cool morning, Fred, the milkman (years ago milkmen had names, wore white uniforms and delivered milk, butter and eggs) rang the doorbell and told my mother the disturbing news that the white cat (he didn't know he was a prize-winning Persian) was over across the road and dead drunk! "It's awful" he said, "he's purring, lying on his back and really out of it. It's disgraceful." My mother ran down the driveway to the mound where catnip was growing.

Catnip is an aphrodisiac that is very good for cats in small doses. It relaxes them, makes them playful and it does change their personalities.

Snowball had definitely changed. He was purring, smiling and having fun, yes, dead drunk. "It's awful," said Fred again, "disgraceful, always so dignified and nice." My mother picked him up, all 20 pounds of wriggling cat, and carried him home. Catnip was all over him, but Fred had found the answer to Snowball's weird afternoon demeanor that even the vet couldn't decipher! He spent his time in the catnip, then, wobbled home in time for dinner – the same agenda as those over indulging in the human cocktail hour!

After that Snowball's outside walks became limited until frost got the catnip. He had to leave the catnip bar alone. Snowball became "dignified" again!

WHOOPIE

By Jean S. Barto

Our search was for a kitten or two. We had seen some but none grabbed us until our trip to the SPCA. Along with several other people, we looked at all the kittens. We walked around then noticed a four month old Tabby alone in his cage, vigorously batting a ball, ignoring the people who passed. As we walked by, he stopped, gave us close scrutiny and then reached a paw through the bars. My husband, Bart, asked the attendant to open the cage. He took the Tabby in his arms. They looked at each other and he said, "This one's for me." I agreed.

We wondered why such a personable feline had been passed over. The story was that he had been adopted as a kitten and returned to the SPCA. Reason: too wild!

"Are you sure you want him" they asked?

"Yes, he seems so sociable," we said. "We really want him."

When we arrived home, we quickly confirmed the first owner's assessment. Our former cat had been confined at night to the laundry and adjacent family room by a four foot high plywood board. We put up the board and in five seconds he was over the top. Confinement was not his style.

Mittens was his former name, a gray striped Tabby with white chest, muzzle and legs. However after our first hour with Mittens, his name was changed to Whoopie and for good reason. He was wild, athletic, sociable and fun.

In his past life, Whoopie must have been a member of the Philadelphia Flyers. If an ice cube dropped, he skillfully stroked it all over the floor; or the Sixers, if you rolled a ball to him, he would lie on his side and bat it back. That game could last ten minutes. Finding him on the fireplace mantle, walking behind guests sitting on the sofa, or in the dryer on top of the warm, just dried clothes was not unusual. He had many surprises.

Hair balls were never a problem, his greatest treat was to be vacuumed with the hand vac, then, thoroughly brushed. Whoopie was not only different but after two friends (both feline authorities) saw him, they confided their assessment to each other, that he was not all domestic cat but possibly had a bobcat uncle or grandfather, something that slept in the woods not on the sofa. He grew to twenty-six pounds of strong, playful cat with big bowed legs and paws like a lion. We really got our money's worth when we had his nails cut since, in addition to putting up a royal battle requiring three technicians, he had six toes on each foot.

Bart retired about the time Whoopie moved in. I was still working and gone most of the day. The bond between Bart and Whoopie grew. When Whoopie was four years old, Bart died. He had been in and out of the hospital four times in the last year, but although Whoopie missed him each time, his eating habits never varied. But the last time Bart was in the hospital (and then for less than twenty-four hours) he died. Whoopie didn't eat for six days. How did he know Bart wasn't coming home? It will always be a mystery. In addition, he bit me regularly for about a month. We survived each other's grief and the gap between us started to close.

Other than that, Whoopie was a good cat, very sociable, cute and funny. He never hissed or spit or growled, but if things did not suit him he would take a little nip. The months passed and soon a year and we both started to rebuild our lives without Bart.

The next Whoopie trauma was when we moved into a townhouse about a year and one half later. That didn't fit in with his plans (big surprise), and he bit me regularly again for a month. Any normal person would have returned him for a refund but the laughs and affection he provided more than outweighed his displeasure. For him I was the only game in town, and for me he added a fun touch to my life.

Whoopie thoroughly enjoyed workmen that came occasionally. He either had his nose in their tool boxes or between the screwdriver and screw. Since he was a strong minded twenty-six pounder and loved to be petted and talked to, they never objected. He also enjoyed any guests I had, however, if they took my attention for too long, he would scratch, not his wonderful scratching post, he much preferred the living room furniture. That really got my attention! The vet was another story. When I would bring Whoopie in for his check up, the vet would say when he saw him, "I'm glad I worked out today" or "I'm glad I took my vitamins this morning," and then call in a couple of extra aides for the ensuing battle.

By and large, we lived in harmony. We played after breakfast. That was followed by a thorough grooming session for him. In the evening, he played "faithful dog" with his nose to the door when I came home, then he'd rush me upstairs to bed. He'd snuggle next to me and sleep like a hibernating bear. Laughs, companionship and devotion sums up our lives together.

At 13, Whoopie became dramatically sick and, although the illness was undetermined, for the next two years he gradually lost 12 pounds, but he was still playful and bossy. Then one day I heard him wailing in a way I had never heard before. I rushed him to the vet who confirmed that his kidney levels were high and his liver compromised. They hydrated him and we went home.

Everyday I watched him decline. His appetite failed He drank very little water. I left extra bowls of water around for him. I tried to coax him to eat giving him turkey baby food. He ate a few mouthfuls. I was afraid to get up each morning for fear of what I might find.

When he could no longer get up, I held a bowl of water for him. Soon I noticed he started to breathe heavily. The vet suggested an ultra sound. I took him in on a Monday morning.. He didn't fight getting out of the carrier like he usually did. He laid on the examining table resting his head in my hand. The vet took him for the ultra sound. A large mass was found and fluid had filled his lungs.

The vet returned him to the examining table where he again laid his head in my hand. She said there was nothing they could do for him and that it was time to consider putting him down. I tearfully agreed. They injected him with a sedative. His eyes remained open. Four or five minutes passed. She shaved a spot on his left paw and injected the lethal dose. In a minute or two, he was gone. I had lost a treasure I'll never get back.

The fun and laughs were gone. The companionship and love were gone. I returned home to a still life-less house. My chest and throat felt like a permanent elevator plunge. My friend was no longer there.

YOU NEVER SAID YOU WERE MOVING
By Lyman Hanson

For much of the 50 plus years we have been married, we have had stray cats appearing at our door. They seem to sense that there is a cat lover in the house (wife). Some have been very sweet, others completely disdainful, and at least one, very pregnant.

I think the most remarkable of our callers was Tom. He was a large scruffy chessie, who started calling on us when we moved to Chestnut Hill. No back door for him, thank you. Only the front door would do. At first, his visits were quite irregular, but then he figured he had a good thing going and would appear daily for his hand out. Everything was very much on his terms. Feed but do no touch, although occasionally in the excitement of meal time, he would brush up against a leg. On very cold days he would sit on the front stoop looking completely miserable, so he, of course, ended up in the vestibule which was heated. By way of thanks, he did not leave any messes.

In time, he became a bit of a nuisance in that he completely intimidated our domestic cat to the point where she would not set foot outdoors, and... she was not a very reliable litter box user!

I thought our Tom problems were solved when we moved a few blocks away and across busy Germantown Avenue, but alas, who should appear at the back door, as we were settling in, but ole' Tom. He seemed quite indignant that he had been left behind. He continued to be a regular caller for a number of years. He apparently found a garage or shed in the neighborhood where he slept, as he was never around at night. He became a bit mellower as he aged. A little pat on the head was accepted and he even permitted a trip to the vet when a paw became infected. He seemed to know that he needed help.

Eventually, his visits became very sporadic and it was clear he was having trouble making the rounds. The last few times we saw him he was almost affectionate. I think it was his way of saying thanks and goodbye.

A CAT WITH A MISSION

By Nancy Puhl

During the years I spent in Belgium, my friend, Paulene, and I lived in many different farm communities where stray cats often just appeared. Many were dropped there by people who didn't want them, and sometimes they just strayed to another house where they hoped to be treated better than at a previous one.

In the nineteen seventies, Paulene and I rented a very large old house that had once been a milk factory in the town of Buvrinnes in front of a large forest and surrounded by many fields. Almost all of the land was owned by the Chateau, and the Comte and Comtesse and family were our proprietaires.

"Paulene, you'll never guess!" I announced. "There's another stray cat in the basement!"

"We'll just leave it there, Nancy, for a couple of hours to see if it goes away. Leave the cellar door open just a crack so he can get out on his own. He probably belongs to someone. That never really is a surprise, is it?"

"Well, he looks quite dirty, Paulene, but you're right we should just wait and see. He might be gone by supper time." Suppertime for us came and went and the cat was still there sleeping on top of the heater, as if he had always been there. "We won't encourage him, Paulene, but he should have some water at least." I took a small bowl of water down to him and then turned out the light. We thought he'd be gone by morning. Well you guessed it, next morning there he was in the same spot on the heater all curled up like a little bird with his head beneath his back paw. I went to give the update to Paulene. After some discussion it was decided that a very small amount of dry food was to be given to the cat to see if he would eat it. Eat it is an understatement. He devoured it immediately, as if it was going to be taken away. At this point he also began to purr and rubbed his head against my hand, which was still holding the dish in front of him. I pulled my hand away quickly. He was so dirty, I wasn't sure I wanted to be touched yet. At least now he had a little food and water. It wasn't as if we needed another cat, we already had nine. Most of them had been stray cats or the kittens of a stray.

By the end of the second day, the cat was still there so we decided to leave the basement door open a crack, and we added a kitty litter box close by. We made sure to leave just a little dry food and water each morning and evening, for we left early for work and didn't get back until almost dark. It was autumn and the daylight in Belgium is very short lived then.

Not only did this cat not leave, but one night when we went to the kitchen to feed the other cats there was an extra cat, not the dirty cat from the heater but a clean, white cat with round black spots on his back. Could this be the same cat? He was obviously accepted by all the others as a long lost cousin. There was no other cat in the basement and the dishes were empty. He had cleaned and groomed himself. The primping worked and, because of his looks and new behavior, we decided to keep him and call him, Domino. Little did we know at the time how appropriate that name would come to be.

Besides the now ten cats, we also had two German Shepherds and three horses. The cats and dogs tended to ignore one another. They were all just part of the family. This new cat, Domino, wasn't satisfied to be just one of ten cats. He seemed to notice everything. It was obvious that he wanted to be in the "inner circle" of the family for he stayed in the living room or kitchen or wherever we were. Our male Shepherd, Zachary, a character in his own right, especially ignored the cats. He wasn't mean to them. He and the female Shepherd weren't interested in those cats and seemed to resent any close contact they had with us. Domino must have made up his mind to change that. He began spending evening hours as close to Zachary as he could get without being chased away. When the dog noticed him too close, he'd get up and move away. This didn't deter Domino. He persisted night after night and eventually the dog let him play with his tail occasionally. Miracle of miracles, this cat and Zachary became such good buddies that they even slept curled up together.

Stray Cat Domino
Teaches Loving Communion
Becomes Mission Cat.

A DEAF CAT AND A BLACK LAB
By Christopher V. Cleary

The leash snapped suddenly as Barron took up the slack. The shock traveled up my arm into my shoulder. As he lunged for the bushes, he started barking ferociously, the powerfulness rivaled only possibly by that of a German Shepherd. While I regained control and braced myself against the mighty pull of a Labrador Retriever determined to secure his prize, I could see a small patch of brownish beige fur through the leaves only inches from the Lab's snarling muzzle. Wow! That was a near disaster for the little creature huddling under the bushes, trying to find some shade on this sunny day with temperatures in the upper eighties.

After completing our walk and returning Barron to his temporary quarters (his owners were staying at an apartment complex waiting the completion of their home), I inspected the bushes. Surprisingly, even after enduring the Retriever's maximum fury, the patch of fur was still in the exact same location. Gently pushing the branches aside, I bent down cautiously and saw a small cat, casually sleeping in the shade. Why didn't he run instead of nearly becoming lunch for a Lab? Something must be wrong with this poor little guy.

I walked to the main office and asked if any apartment residents had reported a missing cat. The personnel indifferently responded that no one had, but would pass along my findings if someone inquired. Upon leaving the office and deciding that this was not an acceptable solution, I carefully picked up the pile of nearly lifeless fur and gave a quick examination to determine if he was injured. The small, extremely light, collarless Himalayan offered no resistance to my handling, and it became clear that he was, at the least, very dehydrated. Returning to the office, I informed the people behind the desks that I was taking this cat with me, and if the owners surfaced they could contact me on my cell phone. With more dogs to walk and it being too hot to leave the already fading cat in my car, a rapid trip home was the only logical course of action.

The phone rang a few times and my mother finally answered. "I am bringing home a cat that I just found, can you take care of him for a few hours while I complete my rounds? He needs immediate help, I think he's dehydrated."

"All right," she reluctantly replied, "but you must have him out of the house within twenty-four hours. He cannot stay here since we already have a cat and a dog."

It is interesting how quickly one can become attached to an animal, especially when the animal is in desperate need of care. The next day the appointment with the vet revealed that the wayward cat was undeniably deaf and, although free of injury, in need of proper provisions. Needless to say, he stayed in our custody and we began to work out some hand signals to counteract his lack of audible input. He learned the hand signals quickly. A week later my new little friend's health was much better and his weight had doubled. As a pet sitter, it's just not good enough to care for your own pets and your clients' pets. Sometimes you also have to look out for the castaways. "Thank you for your help Barron and welcome to your new home, Teddy!"

A TALE OF TWO KITTIES
By Dianne Powell

I have two exotic cats, a Snowshoe Burmese which has short brown fur, shaded to tan and has four white feet. The other cat is known as a "Rag Doll cat" – a grayish white cat with four black feet and a black face. I share their house and we do get along very well. The Burmese cat's name is Max, while I call the rag doll, Tru, short for truce.

About a year ago, I was transferred from San Diego, California to Tampa, Florida. I had made all the necessary arrangements for moving my furniture and other belongings to a new house near Tampa. All that remained was to pack a small suitcase for myself, and to make arrangements to transport the two cats in approved airline carriers.

A couple of days later, after I had obtained the cat carriers, it was time to leave. Upon arrival at the airport, I discovered it was necessary to go through security with my two cats. The inspector wanted to search the cat carriers and asked me to remove the cats. I refused to do so, thinking that they might escape from my arms and become lost somewhere in the airport. So I told the inspector that he was welcome to put his hands inside the carriers to search them more fully. But I said to him, "Be careful, the cats bite!" No internal search of the carriers was made!

Shortly thereafter, we were called to board the plane. I managed to get both carriers in the vicinity of my assigned seat. I put the carrier with Max under the seat in front of me. I had assigned space under the next seat for the other cat carrier containing Tru.

I had given both of them veterinarian approved tranquilizers. Max, the Burmese cat., obediently went to sleep. Not so the Rag Doll cat, Tru. He apparently hated flying and let everyone know. He howled, and he howled and he HOWLED! It was an intensely piercing sound, as if all the devils in hell were after him. I did everything I could to quiet him down but he kept it up and kept it up. I tried giving him some of his favorite food – he still howled. I tried holding him to comfort him. Still he howled. The stewardess came by and asked if there was anything she could do for him besides strapping him in a parachute and throwing him out of the door.

The plane landed. As I waited on line to exit the plane, I heard the flight attendant say to each passenger, "Thank you for flying ABC airline. I hope you will fly with us again. Thank you for flying ABC airline. I hope you will fly with us again." It became a mantra. When I reached her, all she said was, "Have a nice day."

Note: Airline name has been changed to protect the innocent.

CANDY

By Helen Vanderslice

What do you name a cat that is sweet, the color of caramel and vanilla? "Candy," of course! That's one of my favorite candies.

I adopted my cat from Kitty Cottage in Blue Bell, Pennsylvania, after filling out an application and submitting three references. She seemed so coquettish, but it was her beautiful coloring that attracted me. So after I was approved a week later, they put her in her new pet carrier for me to bring home. When I opened her carrier in the kitchen, she dashed out and immediately disappeared! I didn't worry although I searched repeatedly in every nook and cranny, under all furniture and up on cabinets and shelves. How can I not find this cat in my own house? I just about gave up when I noticed a lump under the bedspread in the guest bedroom.

Sure enough that's where she was, so I left her there until she was ready to come out.

We soon became friends and I learned other traits of hers. She doesn't purr and barely meows. She absolutely wouldn't let me pick her up! I assumed since she was two and a half years old when I got her that the reluctance to be picked up was due to an incident in her past. It was no problem until we had to visit the veterinarian for a check up. How do I get her into the carrier? I tried repeatedly to guide her in, lure her in with her toy mouse, but no luck! Finally, I succeeded, after canceling the appointment and making another for two weeks later, by putting a spoonful of her tasty cat food, the soft kind, into her carrier under the table each morning for two weeks. On the day of the appointment, she was inside eating her treat and wham! I shut the door. Success! Well, I've never heard such screaming and scratching in my life. Off we went to the vet's office. When we arrived, I told the doctors of her behavior. They had no trouble in the small examining room. So she got her shot and her nails trimmed and they lifted her into her carrier. Now why couldn't I do that? My nerves were a wreck!

Weeks later I tried to lure her into her carrier again for her next appointment, but she was too wise and I failed; so I ended up calling a veterinarian who would make house calls.

Looking ahead to the time when I planned to fly to California for a winter vacation, I knew I had some planning to do and a few "cat problems" to iron out. My blessed vet advised me to make sure she travels in a soft carrier with me on the plane, not in the airplane kennel. She gave me two tranquilizers, one for the morning we leave, and one for the return trip. Now I'm really concerned about getting the tranquilizer down her throat so she will be sedated enough for me to get her into her carrier. I decided to mash the powder into her soft cat food. It worked well. She ate it and became dopey in a few minutes. After three tries I finally got her in. Now I needed a tranquilizer for myself to get us on our way. She had a quiet and gentle twelve hour trip.

In California, she was a joy. In our screened-in patio and at the big windows of the living room, she could amuse herself watching birds, rabbits, and people. I didn't worry about the trip home, I knew what to do and how to do it, but things never go as planned.

Early on the morning of our return trip, I poured her powered tranquilizer into her food and awaited the results. No dopiness occurred – it wasn't taking effect! Now I wait as long as I can and then take action. I picked her up, she bolted away. I went after her again and tackled her, but she wriggled away. Now I'm chasing her. I tackled her again and grabbed her rear legs. No getting away this time! I think I wore her out. I put her in the carrier and we were ready to go! Except now I needed a couple of aspirin.

She slept all the way home, I didn't, but I prayed a prayer of gratitude! All is well at home. I won't have to pick her up for a long time. Now, I ask myself – "Was it worth it? Do I want to go through this again?" Well, when I'm stretched out on the sofa and she crawls up on my lap and chest, she stretches up and puts her paw gently on my cheek, then I smile and say to myself, "Candy, you're a treasure!"

COMING HOME

By Lois Troster

His name is Boomer, big, brash, brawling. He is a feral cat looking for food and shelter, as the autumn winds blow through his territory. He commands the neighborhood and the colony of ferals wait until he eats or goes into his shelter. He is a fighter defending what little he has. You can see the scars on his ears and face. Yet there's a majesty about him, sitting on top of a parked car in the driveway, he sees friends or foes. He's clever, intelligent, all senses on high alert. His demeanor, a sort of bravo walk, has gotten the attention of the homeowners, and they have arranged a box for him in their heated garage, but even this doesn't suit him, as he selects another old box way back near the radiator and off the cement, higher and more secure.

In the cool mornings, he comes out of the garage, yelling for his breakfast, loud and clear. You have to admire his tenacity to make a life for himself. Then off he goes to unknown destinations, returning late at night or not at all, maybe the highway got him or a trap or another cat. When a feral doesn't show up, the scenario is the worst one. But he is there again, sometimes limping, and sometimes bleeding, booming out his wants.

Perhaps he does have the best of both worlds, "alley catting around" and then the warmth of food, beholden to no one. However, with most feral cats, the end is always around the next corner, and Boomer is no exception.

One night Boomer meets his match, another cat, a dog, or a fox, grabs him by the neck. The wound is mortal. He makes it back and runs for the shelter of his box…and dies.

A sad story, but Boomer, even in his last moments, sent a message to the humans who cared for him and helped him. Making it back was his gift to these people, he showed them how much he appreciated what they had given him – the only home he ever knew. In the end, he made it "home" to die!

****

Note: "Alley Cat Allies" is an organization devoted to helping feral colonies. These are cats that are deserted or born in the wild. They are not adoptable because they revert to nature for survival. The organization members capture them, get them vet care, neuter them and return them to the wild.

Reach them at: Alley Cat Allies
                        7920 Norfolk Ave., Suite 600
                        Bethesda, Maryland 20814-2525
                        240-482-1980

Fins, Feathers
and
Whatever

"Animals feed us, they work for us, they delight us and they keep our planet alive."

Jean S. Barto

A MODERN MIRACLE

By James W. Castellan

Many people have a good fish story. Those of the Christian faith also believe in miracles and resurrection, of life after death. Well, my life experience combined the two giving witness to both a good fish story and resurrection. It was nothing less than a modern miracle.

It all began when my young son, Liam, acquired a small goldfish bowl with more than a half dozen goldfish. They were one of the few animal pets that wouldn't cause his allergies to flare. They were also ideal from a care and maintenance perspective. They only needed feeding about once a week, a simple tapping of a container of small flakes of dried fish food to deposit a few morsels on the top of the water for fish dinners. Maybe once a month the glass fish bowl would be cleaned and the water replaced. Definitely low-maintenance.

Actually, for me there was no maintenance. Liam would feed the fish, Lynn would remind Liam to feed the fish about once a week, and together they would periodically clean the bowl and change the water. I did nothing other than to occasionally notice the little goldfish placidly swimming around doing whatever goldfish do 24/7 in their little bowl of water. Like I said, they were ideal pets, especially from my perspective.

It was well less than a year since acquiring the fish when my wife and pre-school son flew to Florida to spend a week with Grandma in warm and sunny Naples during a most bitterly cold week in February. I stayed behind at our home near Philadelphia to work at my job in the city, saving my precious vacation for later in the year. I was also to watch after things at home.

We had bought our home only a few years before and put in electric baseboard resistant heating individually zoned for each living area, installed external wall and attic insulation and added an efficient wood stove which we planned to be a significant heat source. We were confident that during extended absence even in the coldest stretch of weather the temperature would never drop below 50 degrees Fahrenheit (and pipes wouldn't freeze) due to the earth's heat through the slab even with no other heat. In the traditional age-old battle of the sexes over the home thermostat and temperature, I never had a chance to test this conjecture. Unintentionally, this bitterly cold week in February would provide just such a test and an opportunity for my witnessing, indeed participating in a modern miracle.

After saying goodbye to Lynn and Liam for the week, I proceeded to work longer than usual. When I did get home, I had to check the mail, fix dinner, such as it was, make sure the trash got out and all those little things that Lynn did to make my life so much easier after hard days in corporate life. I never used the area electric heat or even lit the wood stove the whole week. A cool home wasn't a problem for me since I could put on a sweater as the temperature dropped. I was too busy to notice just how cold it was or bother firing up the wood stove during the little evening time I had until I jumped into bed and turned on my electric blanket.

It was the very end of this week and I was beginning to think about my family's return when I remembered I hadn't even thought about, let alone fed Liam's goldfish. I immediately proceeded to do so, picking up the small cylinder of fish food to tap in a belated dinner. I noticed all the fish were floating in the fishbowl belly up with no signs of movement. They couldn't all have starved after one short week. They had to have died from the cold. I immediately checked our home's temperature and fishbowl water and confirmed they both were a balmy fifty degrees.

This temperature confirmation of our unheated house hypothesis wasn't what I was reflecting upon at that moment. Whatever the temperature of the water floating the dead tropical fish, I truly was in really hot water. My mind raced through the homecoming scene now a day away, only to imagine Lynn's look of total censure for not keeping our home a minimum temperature to sustain basic fish life, and my son's total loss of faith in his dad. After a lonely week, I was desperate not to have to face that scenario and the ultimate consequences which I didn't dare contemplate.

While my mind was madly scrambling for a solution, like hiding the fish bowl until I could find time to shop for some new fish, something strange and wild popped into my mind. A fish fact from long ago that I remembered was that in far northern lakes some fish like northern pike sometimes get frozen into the ice and are revived with the spring thaw. Although I doubt those fish were frozen belly up in the ice and certainly doubted that our tropical goldfish had any evolutionary winter survival traits of the northern pike, it was worth a try, right? I did mention I was desperate, didn't I?

While trying to decide how to attempt reheating Liam's goldfish (by firing up the wood stove finally or by putting them in the oven), I realized that I needed some way that would be quick and could be closely monitored. The only thing worse than dead fish would be cooked dead fish (along with my own goose) upon Lynn's and Liam's arrival. Just cuddling the goldfish bowl to my body was not very realistic. That would have taken too long even if I were able to devote my entire attention to these tiny dead fish. But then I thought of the perfect solution: our microwave oven. They're based on the principle of microwave energy exciting water molecules in the food to heat it, right? And I had a lot of water and a good number of tiny fish that needed some exciting.

I immediately inserted the fishbowl into our microwave oven like a large container of soup, saying a prayer of thanks it wasn't a metal-framed aquarium that couldn't have fitted or been safe to microwave. Cautious from the lack of familiarity with cooking anything, fish or otherwise with this oven, I zapped it for fifteen seconds. Nothing happened. I continued for few more fifteen second bursts, knowing that the large amount of water would take a goodly amount of microwaves to raise it to that of balmy tropical seas.

Each time I zapped them, I'd watch through the oven door as I quietly prayed for revival. Nothing seemed to be happening. These fish were sure giving a good rendition of how I imagined dead fish would act in spite of my application of modern technology accompanied with desperate prayer. Every few times I would open the oven door to do a quick finger test to check the water temperature. Other than the water getting less cold nothing seemed to be happening.

But I persevered with additional doses of microwaves, more because it was lots easier to repeat this now apparently hopeless process than to think up another approach that had any great potential for success. Then about the fifteenth zapping, I noticed one fish twitch slightly. A few more zaps confirmed my desperate mind wasn't imagining this, as there were additional twitches in several other fish. Much like Frankenstein, these fish were experiencing spasms with each burst of energy. I took it more slowly and after only a few more applications of the miracle microwaves, the fish began a remarkable revival with most of the fish moving (dare I say swimming?) through the water and beginning to right themselves from their dead, belly-up floating position.

Only two fish never revived. The missing were never noticed by my son when he returned the following day and was greeted by all the rest of the freshly fed fish swimming with a belly full of food and looking happy. But not nearly as happy as I was to have experienced the miracle revival of the fish and, more importantly, to have both my wife and son back home again to take care of the fish....and me. Amen!

A PROPER INTERMENT

By Dick Hudome

My twelve year old youngest son, Greg, went to Florida with the local Boy Scout troop in the troop bus during Easter vacation. I was one of three drivers. While in Florida he purchased a chameleon, which became his pet and best friend. The following winter the chameleon died. Greg came to me sobbing saying, "What are we going to do, Dad? The ground is frozen and we can't bury him!"

Having spent some time in the U.S. Navy, my immediate response was, "How about a burial at sea?" His eyes lit up and he immediately went to the bathroom and made a raft of toilet tissue, placed his friend gently on the tissue and flushed the toilet. He left the bathroom happy, a proper burial, and I never heard another word about the incident, fortunately!

BIRDS HAVE FEELINGS, TOO

By Judy Sheppard

Peanut Butter was a silky Golden Retriever. We had had her for about six years when the surprising event happened. At that time we also owned an Irish Setter-Golden Retriever mix named Dudley. Dudley was made from a different recipe than Peanut Butter. His strong personality intimidated P.B. into following him wherever.

We had just moved and their restricting fence had not been completed. One morning they seized the opportunity, slipped out and took off. After several hours, Dudley returned – alone. We thought P.B. would follow shortly but that was not to happen. We hunted and called but she did not come back. Where was P.B.? Two days crawled by and no sign of her. We were frantic. She was lost and probably could not find her way to our new house.

Finally on the third day, someone found her, read her tag with our phone number and called us. We retrieved her and on arrival home she staggered in, flopped on her special rug under the birdcage and collapsed. The door of the cage had been left open and Teal, our Cockatiel, glided down and gently landed next to Peanut Butter. Teal stroked her fur with her beak very gently, repeatedly and for many minutes, welcoming her back. When P.B. went to sleep, we lifted Teal back into her cage.

Teal had never done that before and has never done it since. And "they" say birds don't have feelings.

HORSES IN SPAIN

By Rose Horrocks

George and I visited a bull ranch outside of Seville, Spain. We were part of a tour group.

We were all gathered in the courtyard sipping our complimentary sherries when a gentleman came riding out on a beautiful Andalusian horse. He put this wondrous creature through his paces for our enjoyment. He finished by riding full speed directly at me. I gasped. Would he stop? He did…inches from me. I was so startled, I jumped straight up. My sherry jumped, too, right out of my glass and all over and the lady standing next to me. We were a mess and shaking, but I swear that horse was so proud of himself.

INDIRA, THE BABY ELEPHANT

By Rose Horrocks

The Philadelphia Zoo had a baby elephant, on loan from India in the children's zoo. Her name was Indira. She weighed four hundred pounds and was a hundred pounds under weight (poor thing).

When I arrived, her keeper was in the enclosure with her. I noticed that baby Indira would take her keeper's hand and arm into her mouth. I was intrigued. I approached the enclosure and Indira came right over to me, a friendly little girl she was. She immediately took my hand in her trunk and then into her mouth. I looked over at the keeper, who was laughing. "She won't hurt you," he said.

"Does she have teeth?" I asked warily. By this time, Indira had my whole forearm in her mouth and was sucking away.

"She has molars but doesn't use them yet as she is not weaned," he responded.

I thought Indira was adorable and felt very honored that she would choose my arm to nurse on. After a while, however, my hand and arm became numb and I decided it was time to extricate myself.

What an experience! I'll probably never have one like it again. I am an elephant lover and it was great to be so close to one of these creatures, to touch its hide, look into her eyes and to have her even trust me. It's an experience I will never forget and will be thrilled at the memory for the rest of my life.

THE CHICKEN ATTRACTION
By Jean Walch

On a narrow road, near a small college town lived a chicken farmer and his wife, James and Ellen Rodgers. To demonstrate their vocation of raising chickens, James carved two wooden chickens which he mounted on a pedestal in their front yard. Ellen was an accomplished seamstress, so she made little outfits for these chickens and changed them seasonally. In winter she had little fake fur wraps and small hats, and in spring she made small capes and colorful bonnets for them to wear. In summer they were dressed in tiny bathing suits and had sunglasses on. Fall had them dressed in football outfits, even with small helmets. In December, naturally they were dressed as Mr. and Mrs. Santa Claus. The local people looked forward to seeing how the chickens were dressed, since Ellen James made several outfits for each season. And it was a local attraction for travelers to the area. It seemed as if everyone knew about the "fashionable" chickens.

One dark night a motorist, driving too fast, hit the pedestal and knocked it down and sent the two chickens flying onto the ground. Of course, their outfits were ruined as they lay in the mud. And at the time, no one knew if the chickens were hurt or ruined. The local people waited anxiously for word of their condition, but for a long time they did not reappear.

Finally, one fine day the chickens were back on their restored pedestal. However, this time instead of their usual fine seasonal clothes, they were all bandaged up with medical dressings and tape. But, they were back and once again would welcome the seasonal changes with their unique costumes.

THE INJURED FAWN

By Bobbie Lane

My daughter, Anne, an animal lover "extraordinaire," was fascinated from her earliest years by the sea gulls at the seashore, squirrels who played in our yard, and loved all the neighborhood dogs and cats. At age six, she fell in love with horses at camp, and has been riding and showing horses all through high school, college, career and marriage. Her animal loving reputation is well known in her small town in the Adirondacks, and often people would ask her to help injured animals or become a foster parent to others. Small wonder that she and her husband parented for ten years a pig who was supposed to be a pygmy pot-bellied variety, but who grew into a five hundred pound house pet! She cared for a beautiful barred owl, which she loved, but who was injured and did not live long. She also mothered a cockatiel bird that drove the household berserk with her screeches, and who, at puberty, had to be assigned to a pet store where there was a male bird for companionship.

There have been numerous other creatures in her fold as well, but the most poignant tale of all is about the very small fawn, born late in the season, and found in the late fall by a year round resident on the lake where Anne lives. The fawn was discovered alive on the ice, but unable to get up to follow its mother because it's little stick legs were splayed out in all directions on the slippery surface. The little fawn was delivered to Anne and Rod's house where they made a nest for her of warm hay in the goat shed. Anne and her veterinarian friend concocted an animal feeding formula. Anne, wearing gauntlet gloves to cover human scent and speaking not a word to prevent verbal recognition and imprinting, fed the infant with a bottle, while the baby stood in a little sling created by Rod to simulate the feeding position of all fawns. This was carried out every few hours for weeks it seemed. Then in the early spring, the fawn ventured outside during the day while Anne was teaching sixth grade, but it returned to the goat shed to sleep at night. This went on until weather improved and gradually the fawn appeared less and less around their property. Anne and Rod felt that they had done a really good rescue job, and did not expect to see her again.

Then, one day in the fall, when Anne returned from her school, there appeared at the end of their driveway near the goat shed, a young doe. It never moved for the longest period of time while Anne, now out of her car, stood and watched. There appeared to be a mild splay to the doe's legs as she stood still, and Anne freely admitted to me that her tears did not stop for some time following this encounter.

After that, the many deer that stroll around their property, and even an occasional bear, just don't seem to have the same impact. She loves them all but her little unnamed fawn will forever seem special.

THE VICIOUS VACUUM
By Joan Hilton

When my daughter, Sue, was about 10 years old, she had a parakeet of which she took very good care ...until one day. She was always very careful when cleaning the cage and always used the vacuum cleaner hose to clean out the bottom. This day, just as Sue started cleaning, the bird decided to fly down, and whoops, he was sucked into the hose. I heard Sue screaming, "I'm not going to go to heaven because I killed someone."

I tore open the bag of the cleaner and quickly got the bird out. He was pretty disheveled and had lost some feathers in the ordeal. We tried to keep him warm and care for him but all failed, and he later died. Needless to say, Sue was pretty upset for a long time about losing her pet bird, and didn't go near the vacuum.

We did get her a new parakeet.

VIRGINIA MOUSE ENTERTAINMENT

By Rose Horrocks

We were staying at a well known resort on the Skyline Drive. Our room was way out on the edge overlooking the Shenandoah Valley...beautiful. There was no TV or telephone in the room. That was all at the Lodge.

Before going to dinner at the Lodge, we were sitting on the sofa playing cards on the coffee table. All of a sudden, a tiny, tiny mouse came running out into the middle of the room, and ran up and down the furniture. At one point it actually ran up my leg and sat briefly on my knee, then ran back down and continued its antics. We loved it.

We went to dinner in the Lodge. The fog rolled in as we ate. We then went to the lounge for drinks and musical entertainment. Finally, we returned to our room. George decided to entertain our mouse (also known as Piddy Paddy) by filling an ashtray with Trail Mix to leave in the middle of the room. He was a good host. He then made a trail from the ashtray back to where we first saw Piddy Paddy emerge.

George went to sleep almost immediately, but I took longer so I amused myself watching Piddy Paddy. He ran back and forth filling his cheeks with all kinds of goodies and taking them back to store. Finally, I fell asleep. When I awoke in the morning, all the Trail Mix was gone and so was Piddy Paddy.

WHO KNOWS

By Andrew Reed

In the beginning of the 1900s, deer were rarely seen in the Boulder, Colorado, foothills. Disease, starvation, predatory animals and hunters culled the herds severely. The open season on animal predators and the restrictions on hunting have caused the deer herds to now flourish.

Now deer on our foothill property are as common as ants, and prance through with total confidence. I will see an occasional black bear but the deer reign supreme.

My yellow Lab, Buddy, is confined in a fenced area close to the house, although his vocal cords show no sign of restriction when the deer romp by. Despite his ferocious barking, the deer will go nose to nose with Buddy through the wire fence showing him daily who is in charge.

Occasionally, I noticed a doe and her fawn sleeping under the protective wooden steps leading up to our front door, an entrance rarely used. As the months went by, I would also notice the pair sleeping in the shade near my shed, 25 yards from the house. They appeared to be comfortable seeing me working around the property. I guess I became very familiar to them. They must have sensed they had nothing to fear from me.

One day, the doe and her fawn, who was now a yearling, were resting again near the shed. I approached to get a rake and they didn't move. As I neared the entrance, the yearling got up and walked toward me. I slowly moved forward. The deer took several steps in my direction. Soon we were about two feet apart. I extended my arm toward the shed latch. The deer closed the gap between us, leaned toward me and licked my hand. Then he turned around and went back to his nest a few feet away. Was he showing his trust, thanking me for not harming them, or just waiting for a handout? I'll never know.

POSTSCRIPT

By Jean S. Barto

The end of this book came on Wednesday night. I typed and formatted the last story, number 60. Now the structuring would start.

Thursday 7:30 a.m., still in housecoat and slippers, the doorbell rang. My next door neighbor and Chris, a dog sitter for another neighbor, stood on my doorstep. Chris held a small, winsome cat.

"Is this your cat? I heard it meowing in your bushes." Laura said.

"No, it's not mine."

A dark Tabby with black back and tiny paws was rubbing his face in Chris' hands begging to be scratched. Chris obliged.

"He's been declawed and the hair on his neck has been rubbed off by a collar, so he is not feral. Someone must own him. I guess he's lost," he said.

I stroked him and rubbed his face. He was painfully thin, full grown but weighing no more than four pounds. Chris put him down and he rubbed against our legs.

I closed the door, hastily dressed and went out again. The little critter was still there meowing in my bushes. Deciding all the vocals meant he was hungry, I opened a can of tuna fish, filled a bowl with water and put them on my front step. He attacked the tuna fish and when I opened the door he was ready to waltz right in. I thought this snack might give him the strength to find his way to his home not mine.

A couple of hours later, I touched the doorknob and my little friend jumped out of the bushes, up onto the five foot wall next to my door. He must have thought, "Goody, the chuck wagon is back." I fed him again (big surprise). He wolfed it down.

A couple of hours went by. Lunch time. Guess who was at the door with another bowl of tuna fish and more water. The minute my hand touched the door knob my little friend (Postscript, I'll call him) was on the wall waiting again. We repeated this sequence about four times. By that time, he was quite full and satisfied, not meowing but he still hung around.

All this activity brought all the neighbors out. (We live in a cul-de-sac of townhouses). Postscript was friendly with everyone, he even walked with me to and from the mailbox, 30 yards away. We were all interested in him and discussed our theories of his origination. I think he loved it.

By afternoon, I had decided that if he was still in the bushes in the morning, I would either take him to the SPCA, or to my vet for a thorough check-up and then home to live with me. By nightfall, the latter plan had won. I would keep him. He had had enough food to give him the strength to go home if he so chose, if not my house was a good alternative. I would wait until tomorrow.

Morning arrived, I ran to the door with the obligatory food bowl. When I opened the door, he wasn't on the wall, wasn't meowing in the bushes and wasn't anywhere around. He was gone. But that sweet little Postscript left his mark. He brought all the neighbors together and took us out of our busy self-centered lives, and gave me my 61st story. I was really disappointed that I would not be sharing my house with him. I pray he made it home, and thank him for the gift of his loving one day presence.

THE END

PETS AND DISASTERS

Excerpts from
The Humane Society of the United States Bulletin

"In the event of a disaster, if you must evacuate, the most important thing you can do to protect your pets is to evacuate them, too."

Have a safe place to take your pets.

Contact hotels, friends, relatives, boarding facilities and local shelters to find shelter for your pets.

Assemble a portable pet disaster supplies kit. Include:

> Medications and medical records
>
> Name of vet
>
> Leashes, harnesses and carriers
>
> Current photos of your pets
>
> Food, water, cat litter pan
>
> Necessary information concerning your pet
>
> Beds and toys

When a disaster warning is issued:

> Call to check shelter arrangements.
>
> Bring pets in house.

Make sure pets are wearing collars with identification and your temporary address.